S0-BYA-089

SHAPE CHANGER!

The White Horse began to stamp his feet anxiously, calling the boy's attention to his hooves, plunging deeply into the precious stones, hooves suddenly transformed into the white-scaled claws of the Dragon. The strange eyes of the White Horse took in the expression on the boy's face as surprise replaced all other expressions. The boy's eyes followed up the Dragon's legs, up his white-scaled chest, broad and powerful, joined at the shoulders by two huge wings. . . .

The Dragon's eyes saw Steve's eyes widen very large. . . .

1 <98

DATE DUE		
AUG 0 2 2000		
MAR 1 9 2002		
AUG 2 2 2002 OCT 2 2 2002		

White Horse, Dark Dragon

ROBERT C. FLEET

ACE BOOKS, NEW YORK

If you purchased this book without a cover, you should be aware that this book is stolen property. It was reported as "unsold and destroyed" to the publisher, and neither the author nor the publisher has received any payment for this "stripped book."

This book is an Ace original edition,
and has never been previously published.

WHITE HORSE, DARK DRAGON

An Ace Book/published by arrangement with
the author

PRINTING HISTORY
Ace edition/June 1993

All rights reserved.
Copyright © 1993 by Robert C. Fleet.
Cover art by Den Beauvais.
This book may not be reproduced in whole or in part,
by mimeograph or any other means, without permission.
For information address: The Berkley Publishing Group,
200 Madison Avenue, New York, NY 10016.

ISBN: 0-441-88571-3

Ace Books are published by The Berkley Publishing Group,
200 Madison Avenue, New York, NY 10016.
The name "ACE" and the "A" logo
are trademarks belonging to Charter Communications, Inc.

PRINTED IN THE UNITED STATES OF AMERICA

10 9 8 7 6 5 4 3 2 1

The piece of paper said:
>   *to help Polish artists*
>   *to give your parents our time*
>   *to help my parents*
>   *to start*
>   *to have fun by working in our profession*

So this novel is written in apology to Stephan and Alina for the hell it cost.

CONTENTS

Here's a to do to die today
At a minute or two to two.
A thing distinctly hard to say
But a harder thing to do.
So we'll beat a tattoo at two today
A rat-a-tat-tat at two.
And the dragon will come
When he hears the drum
At a minute or two to two today
At a minute or two to two.

CHAPTER 1

The White Horse

The gunshots ripped through the silence like a tear in stiff fabric. The No Hunting sign flew into three separate pieces. Only the center, nailed to a tree trunk, remained intact.

A fourth explosion of sound. The center was blown out of the sign, taking a large chunk of the tree with it. From the living bark, sap oozed like blood from the jagged edges.

Lowering his hunting rifle, Bartan bent down and grabbed up the bottle of wine that had been standing at his feet. He took a swig from the bottle, holding its liquid in his mouth, chortling his own self-congratulations:

"Good, Bartan! Good!"

His sarcastic laughter ringing through the lush forest, Bartan raised the bottle to his lips again, ignoring the persistent itch in his crotch, a reminder that he had not bathed for two days. He scratched at the spot absently with his trigger finger, snagging a dirty fingernail on a developing hole in the seat of his pants. He muttered an appropriate obscenity while he worked his finger through the hole and found the right spot to scratch: two days hunting could make a man look like a vagabond, he thought. But he knew that he would look the same after two days at home.

And itch the same. The harsh soap Bartan's hag of a wife employed would irritate the skin of a toad. Karistan

1

was poor in the practical way that allowed few luxuries, and the rural areas found little changed from the days of their grandparents. And their grandparents. The Superintendent might have a fine white Jeep to tool his way merrily around the valley, Bartan gurgled to himself as he finished the last of the bottle, but few others in the valley did. The bottle was suddenly, sadly, empty.

Bartan bent over to put the bottle down on a large rock, a difficult maneuver considering his belt-hugging girth, then turned towards the campfire to make an assessment of his situation. A small bundle of pheasants and rabbits lay near the campfire. Bartan counted each one with a jab of his forefinger.

"One, two, three . . . four . . . five!"

Bartan felt a wave of disappointment sweep over him— only five? With a quick gesture stolen from watching too many westerns, Bartan suddenly brought his rifle to his shoulder and quick-fired a shot!

A tree branch died violently for its sins.

Bartan scanned the countryside along his rifle sight, bypassing the rolling hills and pastures below, stopping with a jerk at the sight of his now-emptied betrayer of a wine bottle. He squeezed his trigger finger carefully—

The bottle exploded!

Not content with these victories, Bartan resumed the swaying arc of his rifle, coming to rest on the faraway stone walls of the ancient crumbling monastery. God, Bartan thought, this country is *full* of crumbling monasteries! He squeezed another shot from his lovely rifle.

A chip of stone flew from the stone walls. Only a chip of stone.

The rifle still at his shoulder, Bartan lowered his sights to the pasture beneath the grey walls: to the center of a small herd of cattle.

As he tried to sight the long distance, Bartan felt his taste for meat, for *real* meat, grow. With sudden inspiration, he put down the rifle and reached into his dirty green rucksack, fishing around with hurried motions until he found the object of his search: a telescopic sight. Fastening the sight onto his rifle, Bartan once again turned his attention to the pasture, to focus in clearly now on the most likely target. In a second he had the cow's head clearly in view. It was chewing its cud in nonchalant ignorance of Bartan's power. Bartan lined up the cross hairs of the telescopic sight.

The cow's sheer stupidity offended Bartan's huntsman's nature. He might be a poacher, but still . . . He swung his weapon away from the pasture and over towards the heavily wooded hills.

A flash of white.

Bartan stopped his swinging aim and began to focus in. Within seconds he was rewarded by the sight of a white horse breaking across a small clearing, quickly disappearing into another clump of trees.

Bartan allowed himself a small choke of excitement: *here* was something! He slowly swung his rifle in a possible "path" for the animal to follow.

"Well, well, Mister Farmer, letting your animals roam into the forest?. . . Dangerous wolves out here—and bears! Could be an—"

A patch of white—Bartan shot on instinct.

The white horse broke into another clearing, then suddenly reared up. Even as the horse rose to his hind legs, the sound of the gunshot came to the animal's ears. He had been hit.

But Bartan did not notice the grazing wound that streaked clearly down the horse's flank. In the brief instant that the animal remained on his hind legs, the horse turned his head in the direction of the gunshot, towards Bartan. Through the telescopic sight Bartan could clearly see the large, strangely shaped eyes. They were almost "Asiatic," reminding Bartan of the portraits of invading Tartars he had seen in the village church during Mass. Then, disappearing from the restricted, close-up view of the sight, the white horse bolted into the next stand of trees.

Bartan ripped the telescopic sight from his rifle and threw it down angrily.

"Damn! Dammit! What's the good of this! What's the God-in-heaven good of this if I can't even kill a horse!?"

Then, through his anger, a threatening thought suddenly sobered Bartan: it wasn't bad enough that he couldn't even decently shoot a horse, it wasn't bad enough that he could only bag two pheasants and three rabbits after two days of hunting—but he had not *killed* the horse! It would come wandering back, wounded, and some God-damn rich farmer would say: "It was Bartan. He hunts. *He* shot my horse!"

Bartan looked around at the debris from his earlier shooting forays, glared intently at a piece of the No Hunting sign that had flown to within inches of his feet.

"Of course I hunt!" he shouted to the silent forest. "That's what a man does—"

A new thought entered Bartan's wine-logged mind. He almost fell as he spun around to stare at the break of trees where the white horse had disappeared. He squinted hard to trace a path that centuries of woodsmen had worn there, followed the distant path up to . . . the Table Rocks. With quiet resolve, Bartan mouthed his apology.

"—a man hunts . . . Sorry, horse: you should have died the first shot. I promise you a quick second."

Holding his rifle by its barrel and leaning the weapon across his shoulder, Bartan abandoned his campsite. It was an hour's walk to the Table Rocks. He did not think that the white horse would go further.

Some of the villagers called them the Crazy Rocks, but the official Karistan maps named the area the "Low Mountains," and the small outcropping of flat boulders in the area near Grodo were designated the "Table Rocks." During the War, a German Occupation lieutenant, a doctoral candidate in Geology, had looked at the Table Rocks once and decided that they represented a very new set of geological structures. Guided by a local woodsman, the lieutenant did not notice the cathedral-like buttresses of boulder that ringed the kilometer-wide area. His interest in the large cracks that let in shafts of light in the "roof" was purely one of annoyance: the striations of light within the maze of passageways made it impossible for him to set the f-stop on his amateur camera.

The lieutenant *was* interested in the signs of valuable mineral deposits he found there, however. He wrote a detailed report on the Table Rocks for his superiors, planning in his ambitious dreams to head the Reich development team that would fully explore and exploit the area.

In a side report, he recommended that the SS round up local woodsmen and have them shot: the Table Rocks were obviously a hiding place for the Resistance. In return for this compassionate analysis, the young lieutenant had his own existence cut short by a woodsman's ax that found its way into his skull one evening while he slept in his barracks. His report was ignored by the Führer, whose ambitions for Central Europe ran more towards the destructive than the constructive. Had the lieutenant lived beyond the month, he would have found himself transferred to the Russian Front with the rest of his unit.

But his edict had had its effect: since the War the Table Rocks had been largely ignored, primarily because those woodsmen familiar with the area had been killed. The villagers of Grodo were too busy putting their lives together to go exploring, although occasional hunters and young lovers would find themselves at the Table Rocks out of necessity. Still, hunting was better further down the Low Mountains. Young Romeos found haystacks more comfortable for their Juliets than the Table Rock caves.

When Bartan emerged from the tree line into the perimeter of the Table Rocks, then, he was treading on unfamiliar territory. It did not bother him: beyond an established ability to follow the horse's tracks wherever they led, Bartan had no further interest in the Table Rocks. He picked up the hoofprints easily in the soft earth leading into a large passage. He was mildly curious to note that the horse was unshod. Perhaps he had been wrong in his reasoning. Perhaps the white horse had no owner. Not a probability, but still . . . Still, Bartan reasoned, better to put the horse out of its pain and hide the carcass from some idiot farmer's blame.

Despite his skill at tracking, Bartan found himself struggling to retain track of the hoofprints on the rock surfaces within the Table Rocks. The recent rain, though, had created a few mud puddles, and those provided enough clear tracks to guide him deeply into the maze. He began to grow annoyed that the horse would travel so far.

Bartan's annoyance ended as he emerged from a particularly oppressive passageway into a large space, relatively wide, open to the sky. There, kneeling at the far end, waited the wounded animal. The red streak of blood was still clearly visible. The white horse turned his strange eyes to look directly at Bartan.

Taking the rifle off his shoulder, Bartan spoke to the white horse in quiet, reassuring tones:

"Well . . . we'll make this close and quick . . ."

Readying his weapon, Bartan stepped closer to the white horse: a single shot directly in the forehead would be best and—

At the white horse's knees, where the blood had dripped down, lay a pool of—jewels!

Bartan found himself frozen for the briefest of moments. Then, without even thinking about the white horse, he fell to the ground, grabbing at the jewels in wonder.

Apparently frightened by the man, the white horse stood up. Bartan took notice of him then.

"Go on, move away. Die somewhere else."

Bartan bent down over the jewels, content at this moment to savor unimaginable dreams of wealth while combing his fingers through the beautiful, wonderful stones. The rearing of the horse caught him by surprise. Bartan raised a forearm in reflex action as he tore his eyes away from the jewels.

The horse's eyes were *very* different from a normal horse's.

The forelegs, pawing at the air, suddenly looked like white, scaled claws!

Everything else Bartan was to see, the *last* things he would see, was obscured by the sudden rush of fire hurling forth from the "horse's" mouth.

CHAPTER 2

Other Prey

The mountains were centuries old, this the Boy had been told a hundred times. He did not know what a century was, but his Father said it impressively, and admiringly, as they made their daily pilgrimage to the tall pine trees and back.

The ground was leaf-covered now, muffling the solid steps of his Father's strong leather hiking boots and his own spring-soled sneakers. The Wolf-Dog at the Boy's side glided silently over the thick carpet of decaying foliage. The Boy took all of this in as part of its due course, his attention focused on the various legs pacing together. Some days the Boy walked with his head cocked back, staring high overhead at the massive trees and branches, at the ancient Adirondack Mountains and the fathomless sky above them. Other days his eyes were straight forward, looking for animals, trying to make his eyes sharper than the Wolf-Dog's. He had failed at that goal so far.

Today the Boy's attention was on the ground, trying to read whatever lessons could be learned from the regular pacing steps of his Father and the 1-2-3-4-1-2-3-4 padding of the Wolf-Dog. He was six years old and stood up to his Father's belt. He was not bored.

The sound of the shotgun was far away. His Father stopped walking.

"Steve, wait here for me."

"O.K., Dad."

He watched his Father's legs stretch into their long, fast-walking stride, swiftly away from him and over the small rise ahead. He did not notice the Wolf-Dog stealing away as well. He reached down to grasp a familiar pointed ear and tickle it between his fingers, planning to explain the ways of humans to the beast.

"Mara, Dad said to . . . Mara? . . . Mara?"

Steve was alone in the forest. With the total disregard of parental advice that characterizes all heroes, he set off in the direction his Father had gone.

It was not a long walk: without the long legs of his Father, Steve had to run to make speed, but he topped the small rise in short time, went down the hill even faster, and emerged into a small clearing that held one sight in particular to attract his attention: the sight of a large hunting knife flashing in the sunlight!

That bold vision once established, Steve noticed in turn the man that was holding the knife, surrounded by two friends, all three of them standing over their kill—a fawn. His Father was facing the three men—and all four adults were distracted by the boy's sudden appearance.

His Father spoke with concerned annoyance:

"Steve! I told you to wait—?"

"Mara left," the boy answered, feeling the explanation to be adequate excuse for ignoring his Father's orders. He turned his attention to the three men:

"Are they hunting?"

His Father answered with an almost embarrassed ducking of his head.

"Yeah. A little out of season, though."

It was probably his Father's embarrassment that caused the three men to dismiss him, for they suddenly looked much more relaxed than when Steve had entered the clearing. The hunter with the knife knelt down over the fawn and began to assess where best to begin cutting. Steve noticed that one of the other hunters was holding a shotgun, leaning on one leg and quietly watching his friend with the knife. The third hunter wore a red hat. He stepped over to Steve's Father, speaking in a friendly tone.

"You know, a few weeks out of season, that's all. They're really getting thick, these deer. Starting to get overpopulated."

Steve's Father began to lean uncomfortably from one leg to the other, mumbling in response:

"Not around here."

"What?" Red Hat asked.

"I said: 'Not around *here*.' We don't have a deer problem. They're not overpopulated around here."

The hunter with the knife plunged it into the fawn's neck. A stream of warm red liquid oozed out over his hand and he shoved out words meant for Steve's Father:

"Drop dead! What d'you know?"

"He knows everything!" Steve rose to his Father's defense. "He's a 'viron-medical doctor!"

The three hunters stared at the boy without an inkling of comprehension. His Father translated with a repeat performance of his earlier leg-to-leg shuffle.

"I'm an environmental consultant. I, uh, check out nature. I *know*: they aren't going to allow deer hunting here for at least five years—especially like that."

Red Hat lost his friendly tone.

"Like what?" he asked with a forward thrust of his chin.

"Come on, guys!" Steve's Father said with a gesture of finally having reached the point of annoyance. "That's a Bambi you've shot there! What is it: six weeks, ten weeks old?! Did it come up to eat out of your hand?"

Steve was struck by the tragic significance.

"Bambi!" he cried.

"Get outta here!" the Knife Hunter spat, cutting into the fawn.

Steve's Father turned away from the men to explain:

"No, Steve, I didn't really mean Bambi, it was just a way of saying—" He stopped in midsentence, turning to the hunters:

"I can't. I can't let you take that."

"But you *said* Bambi," the boy cried insistently.

His Father turned away from the hunters and knelt down to explain.

"I said that 'cause he's small, son. I—"

The three hunters—the fawn trussed and ready to carry—made their preparations to leave. With a sudden explosion of movement, Steve's Father was on his feet again, standing over the fawn.

"You guys don't understand: I can't let you take that deer."

He spoke rapidly, with the near-apologetic tone that he always conveyed when speaking to strangers. The hunters grew restless at his closeness and at the delay he was causing them. They did not notice the rising tone of anger creeping into his voice.

"Look—just go away. I won't turn you in. But you can't get away scot-free. It's my job. Anyway, you shouldn't have been hunting here anyway. You could have hit somebody. Me, for example, or—"

"Screw off!" Red Hat said, shoving past Steve's Father to make room for his two companions lifting up the fawn. None of them were prepared for the violent reaction that followed.

"I said you can't take it!" Steve's Father cried, grabbing at the deer and pulling it from their grasp. It fell to the ground with a quiet, pathetic bump. "You can't take it!"

With a violent explosion of movement, the Knife Hunter sprinted over to Steve and snatched up the boy!

"Get outta here!" Knife Hunter shouted. He made no threatening gestures with his knife, but he held the boy securely. He did not notice the silent padding of feet approaching from behind.

Steve's Father, standing between Red Hat and the rifle-toting hunter, spoke without a trace of his earlier hesitation.

"Put down my son."

Steve, wriggling in the Knife Hunter's arms, saw the Wolf-Dog's thick, muscular forepaws first.

"Mara!"

The word meant nothing to the Knife Hunter. He kept

his attention on Steve's Father, trying to decide his next move. He did not feel the burning, deep-set, wolflike glare the animal cast his way. Mara was a mature bitch: a stranger was holding one of the cubs in her pack!

Steve's Father *did* see the Wolf-Dog, saw the growl rising in her throat. But where the Knife Hunter did not notice the danger, Steve's Father did not care. He spoke with the precision and quietness of great anger.

"I said to put down my son."

"Shove it!"

The boy's eyes glowed with excitement as he cried out again:

"Mara!"

Without further hesitation or sound, the Wolf-Dog launched herself at the Knife Hunter's leg, burying her fangs deeply in the flesh of the knee! Roaring in pain, the Knife Hunter dropped Steve from his grasp.

With Steve safe from the man's grasp, his Father hesitated no longer than the Wolf-Dog had: whether by design or intent, he swung his fist in a wide arc to find the jaw of the rifle-bearing hunter—his hand hurt badly at the impact, but less so than the man's jaw—then he lowered his body and rammed his shoulder in a low, football-style plow into Red Hat's stomach. He drove the hunter back a dozen feet until the two of them went tumbling over in a bruising sprawl.

Steve looked at this jumble of grown-ups and animals with an odd feeling of excitement: he was supposed to be afraid, he knew that, but he could not help wanting to join in. He grabbed up a glowing stick from the hunters' campfire and brandished it like a sword. A likely target presented itself within the moment. Steve thrust his weapon into the large, fleshy target of the Rifle Hunter's rear end.

"You guddem little—!"

A fist hurled angrily by Steve's Father put a quick end to the Rifle Hunter's evaluation of Steve's character.

But the father-son combination gave Red Hat his opportunity to aid Knife Hunter: he grabbed his own piece of debris wood and whacked down on Mara as the Wolf-Dog

rolled hungrily round in the dirt with the Knife Hunter.
She was stunned by the sudden crack to her thick, lupine
skull, staggered. Red Hat brought his impromptu club up
for a second blow—then found his knees cut out from
under him! Steve had swept his "sword" across the back
of Red Hat's legs—finding the weak point of human skel-
etal structure—and the boy laughed to see the adult fall in
a jarring crash to his knees. His Father added injury to insult by boxing Red Hat's ears, sending the man howling in
pain to squirm on the ground.

Knife Hunter did not even try to stand: Mara had regained her senses and was displaying her full set of canine
incisors to the man in realistic imitation of a hunter's
worst nightmares.

Steve waved his firestick sword a few more times, anticipating further battle. But the field remained empty. He
looked over at his Father. *There* was the probable cause
for this end to fun: his Father had picked up the hunters'
shotgun and was pointing it at them. Oh well, a general
had to commend his troops. Steve threw his weapon back
into the campfire with gracious noblesse.

"You did pretty good, Dad."

"You're only talking about a fine, Jim. That's all they'll
get."

Steve saw his father's face turn red: the faces of the
three hunters sitting in the back of the Sheriff's car looked
black.

"But ... but ..." his father sputtered, "what about *assault*?!"

The Sheriff looked at the three crestfallen hunters sitting
handcuffed in his car, then down at the fly-covered fawn
strapped to the hood.

"Jim—*you* attacked them. *Your* dog bit them! Two of
them are going to get stitches, not *you*!"

"I've got bruises—"

Steve was bored by the conversation, he was tired of
waiting around.

"C'mon, Mara," he called, leading the Wolf-Dog over to

a stream where they could both splash water in their faces—although the animal's actions were called "drinking."

"Jim, I'm taking them in only to scare 'em and as a favor to you. And"—the Sheriff gave a nod to the boy and dog—"I have to remind you that we *do* have leash laws. Those jerks don't know it, but they could turn *you* in!"

"Leash laws, Jesus Christ, I—"

A car honking its horn sounds obnoxiously loud in the middle of the Adirondack forest. The dark Mercedes coming down the road let its honks echo into the mountain air three times before coming to a stop at the edge of the stream near Steve and Mara. The driver stepped out with comfortable ease. He was in his early sixties, with very dark hair and a sun-lined face. He wore the type of outfit that Ronald Reagan would wear when he was President and had taken another of his month-long vacations "on the ranch." The newcomer waved across the road to the two men.

"Sheriff!" he called in greeting.

"Mr. Brown!" The Sheriff waved back, a mite too readily.

Jim looked from the Sheriff to the newcomer with a growing suspicion.

"Sheriff, this is *the*—"

"Uh-huh."

Jim brought his attention back to the newcomer, speaking his name like an incantation.

"Frank Brown."

To Steve the newcomer was just another grown-up intruding upon his conversation with Mara: he had been instructing the Wolf-Dog on the finer points of rock-skipping when the old man's car horn had blasted his concentration into fragments. The fur at the base of Mara's tail began to rise, so the boy let his hand fall firmly on her back. He had no hopes: there just *couldn't* be two adventures in one day!

Frank Brown continued to wave to the Sheriff and Jim

a moment longer: it was a "public" movement, made as if he felt watched by others—almost a gesture.

Jim and the Sheriff felt compelled to continue waving, too. Jim began to feel foolish. He asked between clenched teeth:

"What's the great industrialist and country squire of Adirondack Valley want you for?"

The Sheriff, who never felt foolish when responding to rich people, smiled with a hint of wicked glee.

"He wants *you*, Mister Jim Marlowe—and *I* told one of my best campaign contributors where to find the object of his desire."

That campaign contributor was, at the moment, turning away from the two adults and approaching the boy and the wolf-dog. Apparently heedless of the low growl coming from the animal, Frank Brown swept up the boy and held him aloft. It was a "gesture" most assuredly. He raised Steve high overhead for a moment, then lowered him to eye level.

"Hi," he said with as much warmth as possible for a one-syllable word.

"Hi."

Frank Brown nodded towards Jim.

"That your Dad?"

"Yep."

"This your dog?"

"Uh-huh."

For the first time Frank Brown seemed to notice Mara's held-back aggression. Or maybe it was her now-bared teeth. He set down the boy.

"Looks dangerous."

"Not to me."

Frank Brown liked that kind of answer. A careful smile played at the corners of his mouth.

"Good."

With that, Frank Brown promptly forgot the boy and the dangerous animal, turning his full attention to the two men who had crossed the road to join him. His hands were in theirs immediately, commanding the ritual of handshaking and greeting.

"Sheriff—" He turned his attention fully to Jim, the Sheriff as forgotten as the boy and dog. "You must be Jim Marlowe, yes? Frank Brown." As with his earlier wave, his handshaking gesture was held too long to be personal. He focused his pale grey eyes at a spot on Jim's forehead that approximated direct eye contact. It was time to get to the point.

"I have one word for you: Karistan."

"What?"

" 'What' exactly: Karistan. It's a country."

"Well, I know that, but . . ." Jim began to fall into his familiar, hesitant drawl. No matter what he knew about the public Frank Brown, this man was still a stranger. Jim felt uncomfortable speaking with strangers.

Frank Brown felt no such need for hesitation.

"*And* Karistan is a country that very probably has rich mineral deposits—only fifty or a hundred feet below the surface."

Jim was too busy feeling nervous to understand where the conversation was leading. He grunted a neutral "Uh-huh" that allowed Brown to continue.

"*And* Karistan has a recently liberalized government prepared to sign a five-year lease to develop those mineral deposits. You're not keeping up with me, are you, Mr. Marlowe?"

"Uh, mineral deposits." Jim understood that much at least.

"Right: mineral deposits, undeveloped land, a foreign government looking for hard Yankee dollars, a U.S. project—and you. Where do you fit in, Jim?"

Jim had no time to marshal up a response.

"Impact. Environmental impact."

At last: words that mattered to Jim Marlowe.

"You want an environmental impact study?"

And at this, finally, Frank Brown took a breath and stood silent a moment. He looked blankly across the road, then focused in on the Sheriff's car: the three hunters were arguing with one another in the backseat. Brown gave a directive nod with his head.

"Sheriff? Your prisoners—?"

"Oh, yeah, sure." The Sheriff stepped back towards his car, tapping Jim on the shoulder as he passed. "Be there in an hour to sign the complaints, Jim, or they're walking without even the fine."

Brown raised his eyebrows.

"Sheriff, I may be needing to talk with Jim here for the rest of the afternoon. Why don't you just put everything on hold till I get him back to you?"

The Sheriff stopped in mid-road and gave it a second's thought.

"No problem, Mr. Brown." He flashed a wry grin. "You see, Jim, justice better than the law." The Sheriff coughed up a noiseless laugh and returned to his car to deliver the bad news to his guests.

Steve was bored again. Again it was grown-up talk. There had been the promise of a really great afternoon walking around the Sheriff's jail, watching the bad guys he and his father had beaten up get their fingerprints taken. Maybe even see them fry in the electric chair. Now it was just standing here being polite while some old fart talked business with his father. He did not pay attention as the two men continued their conversation.

"To be candid, Jim: No, *I* don't want an environmental impact study. I just want to get to work to help out those people in Karistan and make some money while doing it. But some obscure section of the federal law says that— just because I will get federal incentive funds—we have to file this report."

"The Hardin-Crowley Act, Section Four." Jim had the words out with a speed that his earlier drawling hesitation had left Brown unprepared to hear.

"Hmm?"

Jim smiled.

"That's the law: the Hardin-Crowley Act, Section Four. It pays my bills. I *should* know it."

There was an awkward pause at this juncture, punctuated by a brief comment from Brown midway:

"This somewhat puts us on opposite sides of the philosophical fence, doesn't it, Jim?" Frank Brown had a talent for making a rhetorical question sound like a prosecutor's accusation at a rape trial.

The uncomfortable silence resumed for another long minute—until shattered by a "public" burst of laughter from Frank Brown.

"Good!" He held the laugh a shade too long. "I'm glad to see that that law was made to make money for *some*body! I hate a white elephant—an albatross of a law—for me."

He clapped Jim on the shoulder with a public show of camaraderie.

"But not for you, Jim—for you it's money in the pocket—and that's why I need you!

"For Karistan."

CHAPTER 3

Karistan

Central Europe is, or could have been, the invention of a mapmaker gone wild. Not that the borders are impossible to find—four decades of Iron Curtain politics had made everyone aware of where one country ends and the other begins. But sometime between the beginning of the twentieth century and the end of World War II a number of borders flew up that cut through the hearts of one nationality after another. Poland was "shifted" a hundred kilometers to the west, losing its traditional eastern lands to the Soviet Union, gaining a chunk of Silesia-cum-Germany. One hour's drive from Vienna families suddenly found themselves divided into Austrians and Hungarians, while further south Transylvanians were piecemealed into Hungarians and Romanians.

The problem cannot be lain solely at the feet of the political mapmakers, however. Central Europe—with its rolling pastures cut suddenly by impassable mountains—has long divided itself into a hundred different nationalities. A throwback to the feudal era. The man from one valley might speak a different language, be aligned with a different religious tradition, hold a totally different worldview than the visitor from two valleys away. It makes for colorful cultural diversity within the modern political boundaries. It creates unexpected tensions in daily life. The Austro-Hungarian emperors had been content to let the individual "countries" retain their individualities—as long as they paid proper allegiance to the Empire. The post–World War II regimes tried to impose their socialist stamp upon the various groups, to replace ethnic pride with political solidarity.

They failed.

Karistan had been shaken less by events of the past century than many of the other Central European regions. Poor in natural resources, a region of small valleys separated by the scattershot Low Mountains, Karistan had been virtually ignored by the Austro-Hungarian Empire. Between the two world wars Karistan remained firmly rooted in pre–Industrial Revolution politics and economics. The German Occupation had served one purpose: the Nazis needed to build bridges between some of the large valleys in order to move their tanks and transport vehicles through on the route to Russia. But Karistan—nicknamed "Little Switzerland"—was too strategically unimportant for the Germans to devote much attention to. The Karistan Resistance, organized by the Soviets, was able to oust the Germans at War's end without the aid of their Russian allies. The small revolutionary group promptly declared its allegiance to the Communist cause, closed its borders, and persuaded Stalin that, yes, they were incredibly loyal to him but, please, we don't need your troops and aren't they *more* needed in East Germany, or somewhere else the corrupt West is trying to influence?

Whether Stalin bought their argument was never established. The Soviets contented themselves with sending in ten thousand political prisoners to build a proper Politburo building in the capital, Vavel, and scrape down enough rolling hills to establish an "international airport"/military fueling base. The revolutionary leaders of Karistan were installed as appropriate presidents, premiers, ministers, generals, and so forth—they had to hunt around a little to flesh out the ranks. They spent the next forty years alternately starting new "socialist progressive" economic plans and developing improved methods of stealing from the system they had created. Every few years the Soviets would inject a few million rubles into the system, an occasional road or technical university. When the Soviets began asking their satellite states to stand on their own economic feet in the late 1970s and early 1980s, the leaders of Karistan began retiring in record number, leaving their nephews and nieces in control of a bankrupt political entity.

Outside of the capital, few people in Karistan noticed the changes either way. It was that kind of country.

Jim Marlowe felt uncomfortable in the oak-paneled private study. He had never sat on a chair that cost more than his entire household furnishings. Sitting across an acres-wide desk from Jim, Frank Brown lounged comfortably back in a chair that seemed ready to stand and walk on its own. His right hand rested on a remote-control device, his eyes focused on the wide-screen monitor built into the wall on the far side of the room. It had to be twenty yards away, but to Jim's eyes the screen would have filled a house.

A videotape documentary on Karistan had been playing on the screen. Brown froze the picture on the image of a map. Using a laser pointer, he indicated an area in the Low Mountains designated "Table Rocks."

"Everything is all set, Jim: the preliminary studies are already done. Just make a few days on-site inspection and give it an A-OK. Any problems?"

The job was a piece of cake, as Brown had said, but Jim could feel that Frank Brown wanted him to set out immediately. There *were* problems—

"My son . . . the dog . . . I have to arrange—"

Brown jumped to his feet, leaning across the vast expanse of desktop to grin in Jim's face.

"Bring them along! Bring the dog! Can you go tomorrow?"

"Uh, sure, I think I—"

"Fine, all set." Immediately he was around his desk and heading for the door, but it opened before he reached it. The young woman who had been introduced earlier as his executive assistant walked in, smiling to Jim, a bundle of airplane tickets held out in her hand. Frank Brown had already forgotten about Jim as he stepped out of the room.

Steve did not know which was more fun: playing with the pocket video game Jim had bought him, or the fact that the wolf-dog was sitting at his feet in an airplane, frightening off everybody else around. His father was certainly no fun, reading thick, booklike reports half the flight and sleeping with his mouth open the other half. But, until this last leg of flight from Vienna, the stewardesses had all been mightily impressed by how Steve could handle Mara. They had even invited him up to the cockpit, but he didn't really think he was actually flying the jet when they let him put his hands on the flight controls. He had most definitely wanted to go into a screaming dive, but the airliner had just stayed on its dull, boring cruise through the sky.

This part of the flight—and it seemed like they had been flying for *days*—was sort of weird. They were on a real small jet, but it was only half-full. Everybody smoked, too, which was disgusting. *No* one talked English. And there was no movie!

The city looked pretty neat as they flew over it. Jim said it was called Vavel, which sounded like a dessert, but Steve could see that there was a *castle*, a big castle, in the middle of the city! This held promise, Steve reasoned, because if there was a castle there would have to be knights and swords and, probably (it seemed logical), dragons. Steve had never seen a dragon live, although he saw a TV show once that had some things called Komodo dragons eating wild pigs. They didn't breathe fire, but they were ten feet long. Steve thought that that must be pretty scary, but Jim and Mara were there with him, and that was all there was to it.

He was a little surprised to find that his feet felt wobbly when the plane finally landed. And his head had a sort of stale feeling to it. Walking out of the airplane, Steve knew that he wanted a hamburger. But there did not seem to be any McDonald's or Burger Kings in sight. It was a looooong, boring wait while Jim showed some man in a green uniform their passports, then another long, booooooring wait while some woman in a green uniform looked at their bags—Jim had brought all of his scientific equipment, which always made every airplane trip a problem. Through that mess at last, Steve plopped down on the pile of luggage and tried to close his eyes while Jim walked over to some door where a big letter "I" was painted over it. Jim said it meant "Information."

They didn't seem to be giving his father very much information. Steve had not been paying close attention, but he opened his eyes when he heard Jim talking from across the tiny, single-room-sized lobby.

"I—said," Jim was explaining in slow, labored English, "are—there—any—messages—for—Marlowe? *I'm—Marlowe*. Is—there—any-one—wai-ting—for—me?"

Through the open door, Steve could see a pretty lady looking blankly up at his father. She did not shake her head yes *or* no, just looked up at him. An older pretty lady came up to the door behind Jim, who repeated the syllable-by-syllable question. She plucked some papers from the hands of the blank-faced lady, read them with an intense concentration of her eyebrows, then smiled sweetly to Jim.

"No."

Steve and Mara were swept up in a flurry of arms and legs as Jim began hauling the numerous pieces of luggage and geological equipment across the cheap linoleum-tiled lobby floor, taking out his frustrations in a relief of pointless activity. When they found themselves sitting on their luggage again, this time on the sidewalk under a sign marked "Taxi," Jim breathlessly plopped down next to Steve.

It suddenly appeared as if all the airport had been deserted: there was no one in sight except a green-uniformed traffic policeman standing in the middle of the empty road. The city itself was not far away—down a short stretch of well-paved two-lane road that crossed a strawberry field— but here at the airport there seemed to be a churchlike, quiet atmosphere.

"Where *is* this, Dad?" Steve asked.

"Karistan," Jim answered with a trace of weary bitterness.

"Oh . . . Why?"

Jim sighed.

"I think—I think I have just been given a fully paid vacation." He pulled out a flimsy, carefully folded train schedule from the bundle of papers Frank Brown's executive assistant had given him. At least his time spent in flight had not been a loss: he had figured out the Slavic-Germanic words well enough to decipher the schedule, highlighting his connections with colored marking pens.

"According to this schedule, Stevo, we have ten hours before the train to Mrodo, from where we will then proceed (God knows how) to Grodo—which is *where we must be*."

Steve liked the funny-sounding names Jim was spouting off, but thought he needed to inject a note of seriousness.

"This Grodo place. Sounds pretty scuzzy. Where is it?"

That was a question whose answer had eluded Jim, too. He had found Grodo easily enough on the geological maps—it was between Mrodo and some other town called Dena—and there was a train between Mrodo and Dena. His notes even indicated that there was a stop for Grodo on the train. But nowhere on the schedule did he find the name "Grodo" listed.

"I don't know." Jim gave up. He looked over at the not-distant city. "Do you want to see a castle?"

"Do they have television?"

In semi-short order Jim discovered that leaving the airport would be more difficult than he had assumed: it was Sunday, and there were no taxis on Sunday. Why? Because it was Sunday. Fortunately the farmer who owned the nearby strawberry field would be bringing some of his goods into the city for sale, if Jim wanted to share a horse-drawn cart . . .

Jim wanted. Steve wanted more. Mara thought the horse's legs looked like good game, but the old horse had enough children badgering it in the city to be unconcerned about one dog—even if it was a wolf-dog. Without the accompanying joy of fear coming from her prey, Mara had no interest in harassing the animal. She plodded along behind the cart in a desultory fashion. As the small party approached the traffic policeman on their way into the city, he gracefully raised his right arm, blew a long and trilling note upon his whistle, and halted them. With an imposing snap, he turned a crisp ninety degrees on his heel to face the other way, extended both arms with a forceful show of traffic control power, then stopped the nonexistent vehicles attempting to cross the intersection. Having proved his prowess with whistle and hand, the traffic policeman gave an elegant nod to the strawberry farmer and let the horse cart pass. It was Sunday.

It would have been nice, perhaps, to imagine that Jim and Steve were quickly captured by the charm and Old World aura of Vavel. Instead, both parent and child found themselves depressed by the mixture of grey medieval stone architecture and drab post-War concrete housing. After depositing their luggage at the railway station, however, they still had nine hours to kill. It was only during their long walk through the city towards the castle that dominated its center that they began to sense (rather than see) different shadings.

A mistaken turn off the main road led them through a cobbled side street, where the noise of the boulevard suddenly dampened to a quiet, almost *warm* familiarity. Steve felt for a moment as if he were in the forest once again. They emerged onto the city's Market Square, where open vegetable carts mingled with small Fiats, old women in kerchiefs stood next to young men on motorbikes—Steve eyed these enviously enough—all under the shadow of a heaven-spiring cathedral.

The castle itself was an imposing edifice, its Gothic and Renaissance blendings of power and art a contrast and a complement to one another. There was no television, but Steve discovered the storytelling seduction of the huge tapestries that hung from the walls. Mythological beasts crawled across many of them. Unicorns, eagles, and dragons intertwined with the figures of iron-clad men, weapons gleaming from the flecks of gold and silver that were interwoven in the tapestries' fabric. One image repeated itself in tapestries, carvings, and crude paintings: a black horse, winged, dying. An arrow was always embedded in the animal's chest. The beast would be rearing, on its hind legs only, looking at the knights surrounding it with eyes more full of emotion than the humans'. After finding this scene again and again, the boy began to feel saddened by it, wishing the Black Horse could live. It was no longer simply a "story" anymore, though: Steve knew that, somehow, it had happened.

From the high walls there were two directions to look: down into a courtyard where Romeo and Juliet could have courted one another—or across the Old City below, to the fields beyond the crumbling Vavel walls, where industrial towers stood like modern-day castles in the hazy distance.

The blast of fire from the dragon's mouth looked real: beautifully, terribly, warmly real.

Steve stared up at the cathedral wall—the private cathedral of the long-forgotten kings of Karistan. A dragon had been carved in bas-relief into the very stone of the wall next to the huge entrance door.

"At Notre Dame Cathedral in Paris, Steve, they have a series of saints carved next to their doors—and one of them is holding his head in his hands!" Jim always liked that part of Europe, the idiosyncratic mythology that characterized each region's religious architecture. He pointed out the various gargoyles and saints carved higher up on the walls.

But Steve thought only one other wall statue held as much interest as the dragon—the bas-relief of the wild horse carved as a "partner" to the dragon. It was cut into the opposite side of the entrance door. Both sculptures suffered from the effects of ages of neglect. Both shared a certain immediacy in the boy's imagination.

Mara smelled a new scent coming from the pores of her cub. The wolf-dog felt the hairs along her shoulders begin to itch.

CHAPTER 4
Alta

A fire blazed in the eyes of the peasant woman, a reflection of the wood burning in the fireplace nearby. Her eyes began to close.

"Keep your eyes open. Wide!"

With immediate fear the peasant woman's eyes sprang apart at the firm, professional command in the voice. It was a woman's voice. The peasant woman's face betrayed her fears, displayed the fearful anticipation of a patient awaiting a doctor's diagnosis. The professional voice droned on, the woman's sarcasm masked by her own inattention to the words: she was looking into the peasant woman's eyes, her concentration was there.

"You want my attention," she dully berated the peasant woman, "you give me your attention back." There was a vague foreignness to the voice, a lingering accent from another part of the world.

"You want me to check out everything, don't you?"

The peasant woman nodded tentatively. Yes, she wanted to know everything that could be found, that was why she was there, of course. But then, too, *who* wanted to know *everything*?

"I will look in every little corner, yes?"

The peasant woman nodded her "yes" again.

"That is what I am paid for, yes?"

A small church bell rang in the distance. Without thought

the peasant woman turned her head towards the door and the village of Grodo down the mountain beyond that door.

The peasant woman's examiner turned her own head wearily towards the door to taunt:

"Don't worry, the priest will not find you here. He's never in this village on Wednesdays, is he?"

The peasant woman closed her eyes, muttering a shame-faced "No."

"I said to keep—"

The peasant woman's eyes snapped open.

"No, it doesn't matter." The examiner stood up from her low, three-legged stool. "I'm finished."

But the peasant woman was afraid to close her eyes. She was used to taking directions: from her husband, from the priest, from this—

She looked up at her examiner as the woman stepped over to her door and opened it. The sunlight flooding in blinded the peasant woman for a few moments. Then, her eyes adjusted to the sharp contrasts of brilliant color outside and dark shadows within, the peasant woman was able to focus on the handsome woman standing there. Alta. The peasant woman knew, as everyone in Grodo knew, that Alta was in her late forties. But she looked a decade younger in her face and body, a hundred years older in her eyes. Alta was staring out at the Table Rocks, which hovered a scant kilometer away.

"You eat too many potatoes—and with fat." Alta's analysis could have described a score of village women. She continued: "It will turn you into a cow and kill you someday."

Those were the dangerous words the peasant woman had come to hear. She rose to her feet. Alta turned away from the outdoors and faced the peasant woman to stop her from coming closer.

"But not soon. Take the pains in your stomach to a doctor. You're not dying."

And *these* were the words the peasant woman longed to hear: The Witch had not seen death in her eyes! The peasant woman was ecstatic. She could bear to be sick, but to be condemned to die! No! It was a curse to have a witch in the village—but it was the best: one must know, one must make plans for one's death, one must . . .

Not care just now—she would live! The peasant woman was effusive with thanks as she opened her apron pocket to pull out a handful of currency notes, holding them out to The Witch.

"Thank you, thank you, Madame Alta! I—was worried, you know, and the doctor is not always honest. Is this enough?"

Alta did not bother to look. She knew the peasants' niggardly ways.

"No."

Damn The Witch, thought the peasant woman, she can see into my pockets! She scrambled her hands into the deep corners and grabbed at a few more currency notes, pulling them out to make her original offer look impressively larger.

"Is this?"

"I won't bargain. It will do." Alta tilted her head towards a table and the peasant woman laid the handful of bills down upon it in an untidy pile. Between repeated utterances of "Thank you," she smiled to herself: she had tricked The Witch into accepting *half* of what she had been prepared to pay! Still, to be safe, she gave The Witch a wide berth as she edged out of the house, stepping through the door with her attention still firmly on The Witch.

She walked squarely into the Superintendent.

"Oh! Superintendent." She recognized the moon-faced man immediately. "I'm . . . sorry. I was visiting and it's late now . . . and . . ."

"Yes, it's late now—" The Superintendent gave one of his guilelessly honest smiles. "The Middle Ages have been over for centuries."

The peasant woman looked at the Superintendent without comprehension. She had known him since he was "Little Sturi," born in Grodo thirty-five years before. Now the little apparatchik dressed in a suit and tie every day and pretended he was educated. The peasant woman did not like to talk to educated people. She hurried off.

The Superintendent followed the peasant woman with

his eyes, barely noticing how his ill-cut and poorly fitted suit bit into his shoulders, hips, chest, and crotch. His attention was brought sharply back to the task at hand by Alta's sharp-edged accent:

"Have they been over for centuries, Mr. Superintendent? The Middle Ages?"

The Superintendent would not let himself be cowed. He stepped into her doorway.

"You should be happy they are. They stopped burning witches, too."

"Lucky for witches."

The Superintendent's eyes fell on the sight he had expected to see: the peasant woman's money was spread across the table, stirred gently by the breeze coming through the open door.

"We have not stopped prosecuting charlatans, though."

Alta swept up the pieces of valuable paper with a practiced deftness.

"Charlatans charge in advance. I accept 'gifts' after the fact. Ask the woman, that is what she will say."

The Superintendent nodded in agreement.

"I'm sure she will—if I ask her."

Alta smiled a conspirator's smile.

"Do not ask her in front of the priest, though: you don't want to get her excommunicated, poor soul. Her husband is going to die next week and she will need religion."

"Did you tell her that?" The Superintendent found the hairs on the back of his neck rising, despite his disbelief in The Witch.

"She did not ask that." Alta turned away from the doorway and stepped over to the fireplace. The fire had almost burned itself out. Its glowing embers gave off adequate heat to fight off the chill mountain air entering the house, but cast only enough light to send a pale glow onto Alta's dress. She stared at the embers dully. Against her will, moisture was forming in the corners of her eyes.

The Superintendent stared for a long moment, too, stared with hot, angry eyes at her back.

"I will stop you," he said with cold precision.

"The priest cannot. You can?"

"I will stop you."

And as he uttered those words, The Witch turned her attention from the fire to his face.

"All right: try to make me stop. Try. No one else has succeeded."

The Superintendent felt himself shudder inside, but he fought back the impulse to turn away. He was *not* afraid of The Witch. He was not. And she was not looking into his eyes anyway, not searching into his soul. Her eyes were towards him, but her sight was inward. She was speaking to him and to herself. He wanted to hear The Witch talk. To know for himself the foolish reasons and "spells" she would attempt to throw his way.

"They could not succeed," she said intensely, "because *I am what I am*:

"When I was only ten years old, during the War, *I* did not ask the old women to come with their sons and ask: Will Jan live? Will Gregor come home? *I* tried not to look into their eyes. *I* tried not to see what only God was supposed to know.

"And as soon as the War was over I left. Went straight to Paris. For ten long years I lived there, studied there, tried to be normal there—after all, wasn't this 'witchcraft' just village superstition? I *tried* to ignore the death masks by the thousands that crowded in on me from Paris' beautiful, *alive* streets. How do doctors in the terminal wards keep their sanity?

"In the end, Mr. Superintendent, I returned here. Here, where only a few dozen faces could haunt me. Where people understood that I did not turn away from them, but from myself. And . . ."

Alta felt her mouth go dry. Words she had wanted to say for years had come out, but to the wrong person. Still . . . She allowed her eyes to look outward again, to make contact with the Superintendent.

"I am supposed to feel understanding for you now?" the Superintendent asked.

Alta felt her face flush red.

"This is the one chance I will give you: yes!" she said proudly.

The Superintendent mulled over the invitation, dismissed it.

"Tell me," he asked, "does your daughter appreciate having a witch for a mother?"

Alta felt the rejection sting into her heart. She had thought herself immune to such taunts by now. No, they still hurt. She would not let the Superintendent have the satisfaction of knowing that. She laughed instead. A full, sarcastic bubble of humor.

"I am a normal mother! Would you like to see the corners of my house? No skeletons there, only balls of dust: it is normal, Mr. Superintendent. My daughter is normal."

The Superintendent ran a forefinger along the edge of the table, allowing it to stop at a book laid open on a corner.

"Not altogether," he said.

The book was printed in Braille.

Alta felt the cold hatred she always fought step firmly into her soul.

"That is cruel," she said.

"Yes. Yes, it is." The Superintendent regretted this last taunt. He did not hold the daughter responsible for her mother.

"She does normal things!" Alta said emphatically.

The Superintendent turned and stepped out of the house, saying quietly to himself:

"No, better than normal."

As he stepped into the daylight, the Superintendent—like all children born in Grodo—turned his head to give a nod to the Table Rocks. No one knew why they did this, it was just a custom of Grodo. A habit easy to learn in childhood, impossible to break as an adult.

On the top of a hillside approaching the Table Rocks, the Superintendent saw the figure of a young woman silhouetted against the soon-to-set sun.

"She is normal!" The Witch cried from the dark gloom of the house behind him.

The young woman was holding a large stick. It could have been a walking stick. Or a cane for the blind.

CHAPTER 5

Jewel

Numbers.

Two hundred forty-three, two hundred forty-four.

Always numbers.

Two hundred ninety-seven. Turn right. One, two, three.

Always numbers.

Jewel did not understand why it seemed so complicated to others. (Seventeen, eighteen. Turn right. One, two. Turn left.) The numbers were always there, a clear map in her black imaginings. It did not take any effort (seventy-three, seventy-four) to remember the numbers. Alta laughed that Jewel was a born mathematician. Maybe she was. When she had been very young, Jewel remembered something about Alta and numbers. But that was in France, and Jewel remembered almost nothing else about France. (Three hundred twenty-four, three hundred twenty-five.) That was almost twenty years ago. A lifetime practically.

Jewel felt the sun boring in on her taut cheekbones: it was lower in the sky now, no longer warming her forehead. Soon the sun would be cold altogether, taking its warmth from her. Jewel had read poems about glorious sunsets, with "bold palettes of red washing over mine eyes/filling my senses with colour." Pah! "Filling my senses" indeed! Jewel did not have to be a poet to understand that too many lines were wasted on what one could see, not on what one could *feel*. And *hear*!

And taste.

And smell.

No one filled their senses the way a blind person did. As she stepped along the strange path (four hundred three, four hundred four) Jewel felt it map itself out across every fiber of her senses, save the one denied her. Here (four hundred fifteen) was a small, dead chill—ages-old stone holding the dampness of centuries—a flash of warmth and breeze (four hundred nineteen) and she had found the space between two towers of rock. This part of the Table Rocks was new to her, but only because she had never come from this direction before. (Four hundred fifty-seven, four hundred fifty-eight.) The numbers and sensations drew a gridwork of impressions on her memory, became familiar.

Jewel used the long, hand-carved branch she held in her hands like a biblical staff, alternately feeling the footpath in front of her and using it for support—a third leg—up and down the steeper inclines. Occasionally the stick became a striking weapon, knocking aside new-grown branches that stuck out on the paths. At this moment (five hundred two) the staff struck empty space instead of a path: she was at one of the cliff edges of the Table Rocks, overlooking the village. Alta's house would be halfway down the mountainside. Jewel paused at the cliff's edge for a moment to let Alta see her if she was on the lookout.

The numbers receded into the back of Jewel's thoughts once again. She knew this spot. There was no need to concentrate upon the way home. Back-stepping a rapid nine count, Jewel retraced her steps to a branch off of the path that she knew would lead down to the house. A long stretch of chill convinced Jewel that it was growing too late to be out walking. The sun would have to have dipped very low in the sky to cast such deep shadows without warmth. She had no fear of the darkness, but the cold was no friend. Jewel felt the last golden rays of sunlight with renewed appreciation when the path turned to an east-west angle.

And she heard the scuffling sounds that accompanied

her footsteps. Oh well, Jewel thought, there is no one who owns these mountains, they are not mine alone. She expected the scuffling sounds to melt into familiar foot sounds momentarily. She knew most of the mountain regulars, what few there were. Bodek favored his right heel with a half-step to that side. Drunk Bartan was always shuffling his feet. Stein walked catlike, but Jewel always recognized him. Jewel liked Stein, with his crazy, harmless talk and his always-carried "collection" closed away in its flat case. She had never met any of them in the Table Rocks before.

The scuffling sounds did not grow more distinct. This annoyed Jewel. Petulantly she stopped in mid-step and turned to face the following sound.

There was no sound.

Oh, yes, Jewel thought, these are the stupid games the village children like to play. Well, I can wait them out.

There was no sound.

Jewel began to doubt herself. The scuffling sound had been unfamiliar. Perhaps it had been only a distortion, an echo of rustling leaves bounced too many times among the rock walls. Certainly no child would be up in the Table Rocks, and no adult would play such a game. Jewel began to walk again.

A moment later the scuffling sound resumed.

Jewel slowed her pace. After a moment's delay, the scuffling sound slowed as well. But it was closer now. Without apparent concern, Jewel continued down the familiar path, turning the sharp curve of rock corridor and coming to an abrupt halt in the dark shadows cast there. Safe in her darkness, Jewel turned to face the unrecognized pursuer.

The scuffling sound stopped. Whoever was making it had halted only a few meters from Jewel.

"I don't like being followed," Jewel said in the pursuer's direction, sarcasm edging the tone of her words. "I can take care of myself."

Jewel expected to hear an embarrassed villager stuttering apologies, or a drunken hunter mumbling and pushing past. The Voice that answered was neither.

"Then let me pass" were his quiet words. No apology, no embarrassment.

No threat.

No annoyance.

The words were almost a whisper, yet strong and clear.

It was Jewel, then, who felt awkward. Of course: she was slow, blocking the narrow path, and someone had been politely looking for an opportunity to pass without disturbing her. Had she been singing to herself out loud again? Jewel did not remember.

She stepped to one side of the path. A moment later the sound resumed—only now it was clearly a footstep. A horse's footstep, to be exact. Jewel stretched out her hand and touched its flank.

The rider was apparently leading the horse, his human footsteps lost in the louder sound of the horse's hooves clicking on stone, for Jewel touched only the heaving sides of the animal. There was no rider's leg to touch. No saddle. Jewel liked the thought of a horse ridden without a saddle.

"Your horse feels very strong. I am sorry to have slowed you down."

The horse's steps had nearly disappeared around the next curve of the path when the Voice answered:

"Someday I will let you ride with me."

CHAPTER 6

Grodo

The village of Grodo was not really that small, it's just that there was no particular reason for anyone in Karistan (or the rest of the world, for that matter) to go there. As a consequence, the main road into and out of the village was in a constant need of general repair—not to mention paving—and the concept of more than once-every-two-days bus service was an idea whose time had not yet arrived.

A village.

A town, a city.

A place to live.

Grodo fit into a familiar pattern for Central European socialist countries. Its one main street boasted a dozen off-shoots into dark alleys and dusty side roads. Located on the side of the Low Mountains, Grodo could not boast of a central square—geography had forbidden that standard of medieval town planning—but it did look proudly to its cathedral, the Basilik of St. Georgi.

Grodo had been lucky in some time six hundred or seven hundred years past. In that era, the nearby Monastery of St. Mikail housed a powerful order of returned Crusader-friars. Though its walls were crumbled ruins now, the Monastery had been a local power center, lending its fighting monks to the Karistan nobility in return for contributions to its ever-growing land base. Grodo was the nearest village, a legacy to the Monastery from a childless duke or count. (Or maybe not even a legacy at all—recent socialist history had described the relationship as an "imperialistic takeover by the hypocritical religious zealots of the Order of St. Mikail.") The Order built the Basilik in the center of Grodo, setting up the town as a sort of medieval commercial outlet in order to leave the Monastery proper untouched by mundane concerns.

The town of Grodo flourished as long as the Order did. Nothing, of course, grew large in such a mountainous region. The Monastery walls were pushed to their extreme, and then satellite abbeys were established at the periphery of the Order's domains. For a short while Grodo became a major stopover point for merchants crossing the Low Mountains. But crops could not grow in abundance on the steep hills nearby. There was only one-way traffic on the river: downstream *away* from Grodo. It was a false prosperity. When the Order's power diminished, Grodo returned to village status.

It was a rather abrupt transition, however. The Order of St. Mikail, unlike its brother orders the Templars and the Teutonic Knights in other parts of Europe, did not engage in a deadly war against a nationalistic nobility. Their religious legacy was not demeaned by a series of power plays. The abuses of the Order may have been legion, but they were in keeping with the times. Instead, the Order of St. Mikail committed a form of structural "suicide" in the cause *of* nationalism. Caught between the ambitions of Rome and the growing identity of Karistan, the Elders of the Order opted to cast their fate into the hands of God.

The Tartars had grown more powerful, joined now to the ranks of the Ottoman Turks. Their invading army for this generation of conflict was more organized than ever, with supply lines efficiently carrying their strong horsemen over the Low Mountains.

The nobility of Karistan, clamoring for "national" rights, was in typical disarray. Safely behind the thick Monastery walls, the Order of St. Mikail could have ridden out the storm, perhaps even have negotiated a separate peace with their familiar Tartar enemies. But the Elders of the Order had another plan: fight *outside* the walls and let God decide their Order's fate.

It was not the foolish decision of old men. The stakes were clear: Should the Order be victorious, then Karistan would effectively be theirs (i.e., Rome's) *without* Christian fighting against Christian. Should the Order fail, then God had indicated that He did not want Rome to conquer.

The results of this strategic decision showed that God had an ironic sense of humor. The Knights of the Order of St. Mikail set out from behind their Monastery walls and charged deeply into the heart of the invading Tartar army. The battle was fierce and long. In the end, the Tartars were defeated and Karistan saved for Christendom. Unfortunately the only Christians surviving to make that claim were a handful of bedraggled Knights of the Order—and the fresh, newly created Army of the King, a hastily recruited band of knights and peasants. Under the nominal command of a clever baron named Lek, who proclaimed himself King in Vavel, in quick order the Army commandeered the Monastery, thanked the heroic defenders of Karistan, and accidentally allowed the structure to catch fire. Stone walls burn slowly, so it was with some luck that the Army found time to pull down large sections of the walls before the fire could spread to the surrounding countryside.

Still, the Order had saved the country. Since King Lek proved to be a drunkard (and childless to boot), the Order of St. Mikail lived on in Karistan history as the first defenders of the nation, rather than as the last bastion of feudalism. Even the past forty years of "socialist revisionist historical retrospection" had been unable to shake the ordinary Karistan citizen's belief in that.

This brief interpretation of the history and geography of Grodo was not in the hastily sketched traveler's guide that Jim Marlowe was reading, but he had no trouble in filling in the gaps between narrative aridity and probable fact. Jim actually had done very little reading for the past two hours: the jostling of the truck made him nauseous enough without adding eyestrain to the list of complaints.

It had been a bad trip from Vavel. The concept of a sleeping car on overnight trains apparently did not apply to travel within the borders of Karistan, at least as a working proposition. While rumors of such a car had invaded the train schedule at the Central Station in Vavel, Jim had been unable to find any tickets. His fallback plan—to pay a conductor directly for access to a sleeping car—was met with an incredulous stare: did not the Mr. Marlowe from New York know that sleeping-car tickets were sold out *weeks* in advance?

That was not the only good news. As Jim trudged past the seating compartments, dragging along a sleepy son and a sullen dog, he discovered that buying passage on a Karistan train did not include the guarantee of a seat. His only satisfaction, sitting in the crowded aisle outside the seating compartments, was when the conductor tried to charge him extra for his many bags that were clogging the way: Jim let Mara growl and show her teeth in a manner that persuaded the conductor to try his extortion routine elsewhere.

Boarding was the easy part of the trip. The train was a milk run, traveling at a speed of forty kilometers per hour and stopping (or so it seemed to Jim) every fifteen minutes. Every stop involved the passage down Jim's aisle—he was beginning to feel possessive—of at least two loudly talking people: one departing, one oncoming. Strangely, there never seemed to be any seats freeing up in the compartments. But, then, it was growing ever more difficult to see into the compartments as the inhabitants closed the curtains and locked their doors. Just before arriving at his stop (at 4:30 A.M.), Jim peered into a nearby compartment when the door was opened for a moment: there were only two passengers inside, stretched out comfortably on the bedlike seats that faced across from each other.

As the schedule had indicated at Central Station, there was no stop in the village of Grodo. There was, however, a stop *for* Grodo. It was a level stretch of platform with a half-shelter built next to the rails. At one end of the platform was a metal sign indicating the rare visits from the train. At the other end was a metal sign indicating the slightly more frequent visitations of the bus service that connected the traveler to Grodo and villages beyond. The bus would not come for another twenty-eight hours. Jim rediscovered some obscenities he had forbidden Steve to speak.

The boy and the wolf-dog found the place interesting: both had slept curled up among the bags during the train ride and responded to the crisp fresh morning air with typical expressions of energy. Jim did not share their enthusiasm, despite the fact that the newly risen sun had given a heart-catching dazzle to the dew-covered surrounding fields.

Breakfast consisted of a large Toblerone duty-free chocolate bar each, Steve enjoying this repast immensely, while Mara padded out into the fields to find a convenient mouse or squirrel to munch on. Jim remembered why he had discontinued caffeine coffee with such reluctance. He tried a series of pain-inducing stretching exercises while he considered travel options.

Given his brief experience with the ways of Karistan, there was no way that he was going to sit at this platform to wait for a bus that promised no guarantee of ever arriving. Jim was definite on that point. Walking? Twelve bags, a boy, and a dog up thirty-two kilometers of mountain road argued against the option. There was at least one farmhouse in sight . . . The concept of a hot breakfast held great appeal to Jim's imagination. Perhaps a room overnight? ("Yankee dollars, señor"—Jim regretted that he spoke only Spanish.)

He waited for an hour before hiking the half kilometer to the farmhouse, only to discover that the inhabitants had been up and about since before the train arrived. Breakfast had been eaten long ago. But the farmer's wife gave out thick slabs of dark bread and cups of hot scorching tea that seemed to reach down to Jim's very toes and wake him up.

She gave Jim a half-loaf of the magical food to take back to Steve and Mara at the platform. A half hour later, the farmer drove up to the platform in a vintage World War II Lend-Lease truck. The front seat next to the driver was filled with spare engine parts, but he was driving in the right direction with a load of hay and the Americans were invited to ride in the back. Despite a distinctly rank smell to the fodder, the offer was accepted.

Jim closed the traveler's guide and tried to erase the last day's frustrations from his mind. It was time to gather some fresh impressions of Karistan as the truck made its lurching way towards Grodo. He considered pointing out various sights of interest to Steve, but the boy was deeply involved in a Karistan comic book. Mara had burrowed into the hay and was curled up asleep. Jim gave up thoughts of culture and first impressions: he fell into a comfortable doze.

He was vaguely aware that the truck was passing through several small villages. Jim wondered if the farmer had ever actually *been* to Grodo. A shouted query through the driver's side window did not elicit an encouraging response, primarily because the farmer had borrowed Steve's Walkman portable tape player and was busily drowning out the world in a barrage of preteen American pop music. There was a village up ahead that roughly corresponded to where Grodo should be. Jim stood up in the back of the truck and tried to see through the dust rising from the road as the truck rumbled past.

The first person Jim saw was an old woman kneeling before a roadside shrine to the Virgin Saint. (About the "Virgin Saint" the traveler's guide was unclear: there had been several virgins who were saints in Karistan history, and a slew of them had become national symbols. The countryside was dotted with tributes to the assorted regional Virgin Saints.) The truck slowed down as it reached the outskirts of the village, giving Jim the opportunity to call out to the woman in his guidebook phrases:

"Is this Grodo?" he shouted.

The old woman stopped crossing herself in mid-slice-through-the-air to answer in a hoarse, nasal voice: "What?"

"GRODO?"

The Superintendent was stepping out onto the street, carefully closing the front door of the Village Committee Meeting Hall behind him. It was a modern building—as opposed to the old-fashioned Basilik across the road. Hence, it was an ugly concrete and brick structure instead of the handsome stone and mortar of the traditional village buildings. The Superintendent was carrying his pile of official documents in a fussy stack when he heard the loud voice calling its way down the road. He turned to see an apparently crazy foreigner standing in the back of a truck and shouting the word "Grodo" at every villager the truck passed. The Superintendent realized immediately: this must be the American official he was expecting!

The truck was just passing the Village Committee Meeting Hall. With a leap onto the road that sent his papers scattering behind, the Superintendent shouted at the farmer driving the truck: "Stop! Stop!" But the farmer was immersed in his Walkman music, the earphones shielding his attention from all intrusive sounds of the real world.

"Stop the truck, you pigass!" the Superintendent yelled, running frantically to keep up with the truck.

Jim, who had been shouting his queries on the other side of the truck, heard the breath-starved cries and turned to see a plump figure rapidly losing ground to the mechanical power of the truck.

"Grodo?" Jim cried to the running figure.

"You're *here*, Mr. Marlowe! Make him stop!" The Superintendent's words came out in short, explosive gasps.

"I don't think he knows we're here!" Jim shouted to the receding figure. "I told him there'd be a sign!"

"There's no sign!" the Superintendent yelled, knowing that his lungs would soon burst.

"Why?" Jim yelled back.

"BECAUSE THERE'S NO SIGN!" the Superintendent screamed with his last memory of breath. There was a

long story behind why there was no sign, but the Superintendent did not think that this was the time to tell it.

At one end of Grodo sits the shrine to the Virgin Saint. At the other end sits the village restaurant-cum-bar, a polar opposite in terms of function, equally popular in terms of village needs. At the moment the Superintendent was trying unsuccessfully to halt the truck, two erstwhile poachers, Georgi and Johann, were stepping out of the bar. They were disgruntled poachers. Their displeasure had two sources. First, they had had a very bad week finding game. Second, they had just been informed for the millionth time that the bar was not allowed to serve beer before noon. Even though Georgi and Johann had threatened to bash in the owner's head with their thick walking sticks, he would not serve them.

It was at that very moment, then, that they heard a deep grinding sound, followed by a mechanical hiccup, and turned to see a farm truck loaded with hay dive into and out of a pothole—sending its cargo, plus a man, a boy and a dog, bouncing into the air. The ensemble appeared to land back into the truck in one piece, but not without a considerable rescrambling of positions. The boy began pounding on the roof of the truck cab, while the man seemed to be having difficulty untangling himself from the dog. Behind them all, the Superintendent was chugging down the road, calling for the truck to stop.

"Look at the fat little goat trying to catch a truck!" Georgi laughed. He had never liked Little Sturi as a boy, liked him even less as a rear-kissing grown-up apparatchik. Still, "Mr. Superintendent" had pull. Better to combine a taunt with a helping hand—that way you could ruffle Little Sturi's feathers and still be safe.

That thought in mind, Georgi stepped out into the middle of the road—and right in front of the oncoming truck. Despite being lost in his music world of strange American tribal rhythms, the farmer could not help but see the sudden obstacle. He jammed on his ancient brakes, bringing the truck to a jolting stop. The truck actually "hopped" over the last few cobblestones of the main street before coming to a halt, its brakes locked solid. When it came to its complete stop, half of the hayload tumbled down the back—carrying with it Jim Marlowe—and onto the pursuing Superintendent.

This development was too good to be true! Georgi and Johann roared with renewed spirit at the ridiculous sight of the Superintendent trying to swim his way to the surface of the loose hay that had spilled from its wired bales. They even ignored the pointed obscenities of the farmer, who intended to let Georgi, Johann, and the village of Grodo know about Georgi's sexual deficiencies in no uncertain terms. For his part, the farmer quickly recognized that Georgi was twice his size—and so kept his complaints verbal and safely inside the locked door of his truck.

Making their way to the rear of the truck, Georgi and Johann grabbed roughly at the Superintendent's hands, pulling him up out of the hay to the very definite accompaniment of attempts to tear his suit in the process.

"Come on, stand up, Little Caesar!" taunted Johann.

The Superintendent attempted to pull his hands away, but found himself caught up in a coughing spell from the dust of the hay. Georgi turned his attention to the emerging form of Jim, berating the Superintendent sarcastically:

"This is how you greet visitors to our 'city,' Mr. Superintendent?"

"Leave him alone," Jim coughed. He looked up at the truck, trying to focus his dust-filled eyes. "You all right, Steve?"

The boy was sitting comfortably up on the truck, settled on top of a precarious pyramid of still-bundled hay bales.

"I'm OK, Dad!"

But Georgi's and Johann's "feelings" were hurt.

"What is this kind of people you are bringing here?" Johann demanded, grabbing the Superintendent roughly by the biceps.

"Leave him alone—" Jim coughed again. He could not bring himself to stand up yet. "Leave *us* alone!"

This would not do, Georgi thought. It was no good for foreigners to come in thinking they could insult honest

poachers. He turned to deliver an advisory kick to the foreigner when—*yelp!*—a large dog suddenly emerged from
the hay at his feet!

Georgi raised his thick walking stick in a threatening
gesture towards the animal: "What the—!"

"Don't—" Jim cautioned.

Johann raised his own walking stick: "I'll tell you, you
don't tell me!"

"Don't you hurt my dog!" yelled Steve, standing now
on his pyramid of hay bales.

The poachers ignored the boy—which was a mistake in
retrospect, since he shoved a fifty-pound specimen of hay
baling off its pyramid and crashing down onto Johann's
skull. Johann's knees bent accordingly.

Georgi, of course, did not have to look at his friend's di-
lemma, but he did, and he joined his friend in falling down
shortly thereafter as Jim took advantage of the poacher's
inattention to business by kicking Georgi's feet out from
under him.

Meanwhile, back at Johann, Mara suddenly found herself incredibly close to the hand that had only a moment
earlier raised a stick to strike at her. The invitation was obvious, and the wolf-dog sank her teeth into the soft wrist
with relish. Johann lost interest in holding onto his thick
walking stick. The Superintendent grabbed it away with an
unfortunate swak to Johann's ribs in the process.

Jim was less delicate with Georgi: he stepped on the
poacher's wrist and wrenched the walking stick away with
a burst of anger that left no room for coughing in the dust.

"Look out, Dad!"

Jim turned, wide-eyed, to see his son pulling at a key
support of the remaining hay-bale pyramid up on the
truck. He had enough wits left to shove the Superintendent
out of the way, then narrowly escaped the falling, collid-
ing, tumbling onslaught of hay bales that landed heavily
on the two unfortunate poachers lying prone on the
ground.

As the dust cleared, Jim was able to make out that his

son had had a little help: the farmer was up with Steve, wiping his hands with satisfaction at a job well done.

Then, in heartfelt sincerity, the farmer began applauding himself. A moment later, the Superintendent joined in, feeling pleased as well. Steve thought that clapping was a good idea, too. By the time Jim joined in, a handful of villagers were standing in a circle, looking with smiles at the pile of hay bales left in the middle of their main road. They were all applauding. It was a good way to greet a stranger.

CHAPTER 7
Settling In

"You should have used the telephone, Mr. Marlowe. I would to send a car."

Jim smiled politely at the Superintendent's belated offer. He had caught a glimpse of the "official" World War II–vintage Jeep sitting out in the dusty alley next to the Village Committee Meeting Hall. Jim liked his family too much to put them all at such a risk of life and limb. He shivered slightly at the thought of a trip from Vavel in the decrepit vehicle.

Or perhaps it was a shiver from the cold. The concrete frame of the Village Committee Meeting Hall kept out the wind and dust, but it carried a dampness within its structure that the inadequate central heating system could not control. Jim felt his head growing hot from the stuffy air of the building, while his feet seemed to soak in the stone cold from the floor. He looked jealously out a window to where Steve and Mara were standing in the warm sunshine. Steve was comfortably showing a pocket video game to a peasant boy who did not comprehend what he was looking at.

The Superintendent handed Jim a glass filled with hot, bitter tea, an inch of coarse-grained sugar settled onto the bottom. Jim felt obliged to keep up his end of the conversation.

"I didn't know who to call." He was grateful that the

Superintendent spoke English. "Besides, I just gave this farmer twenty dollars and he said he'd drop me off."

"Twenty dollars!" the Superintendent yelped. Jim jumped at the note of alarmed reproach in the Superintendent's voice.

"Not enough?" he asked timidly.

The Superintendent shoveled a fistful of sugar into his own glass of bitter tea and looked pitifully at Jim.

"Ours is a good system, one that gave me an education, one that builded up our country after War. I live comfortably—by our village standard. I earn equal to your American thirty dollars each month."

Jim spent the next few minutes commiserating politely with the Superintendent. His thoughts, however, rolled deliciously over the realization that the per diem MERCO was paying him would go a lonnnng way further than he had anticipated. Jim looked forward to making a tidy side profit on this job. All legal.

"Who was the welcoming committee?" he asked, by way of heading off a probable loan plea from the Superintendent. Some portions of his travel guide had been very specific about Karistinian customs.

Jim's question had its local counterpoint several times over the next two days, asked specifically within the context of the following conditions:

Setting: the window seat of the Grodo restaurant and bar
Time: anytime of day from noon until closing
Participants: two alleged poachers by the names of Georgi and Johann, plus any unwilling resident of the village who happened to be within earshot
Question: "What in the Virgin Saint's lost honeypot are the Americans doing in Grodo anyway?" (or variations thereof)

The cause of such caustic commentary was not—as might be imagined—simply Georgi and Johann's bitterness over their inglorious introduction to the Marlowe family.

That hurt, but the other villagers sympathized too readily with the victors for the two natives to call upon the incident to much useful effect. (Georgi had tried, but when even the stupid old woodsman Stein laughed at him, he knew it was a lost cause.)

Now, exposed to the insidious American ways for two days, the villagers of Grodo were ready to wonder aloud at their customs—and Georgi and Johann were ready to add the righteousness of bigotry to the local voice.

Perhaps there would have been less wonder if Jim Marlowe had gone directly up to the mountains and begun his review of the MERCO documentation vis-á-vis environmental impact. The villagers of Grodo still would not have known what he was doing, but they would have seen him working. That they understood.

Instead, Jim had decided to let his "travel clock" adjust to Karistan time. The Americans were put up in the opulent State Country House just outside the village—a "donation for exclusive use" by the lately dismantled Central Committee of Vavel, who liked comfort when they went hunting in the Low Mountains. Among the many tons of professional gear Jim had dragged with him could also be found a dismantled portable bicycle. Within hours of arrival, the village of Grodo was treated to the sight of a polyester-suited American environmentalist jogging down their main road, accompanied by his bicycling six-year-old son and what appeared to be a wolf-in-dog's training; two of the three wore sweatbands and Walkman cassette players clamped to their heads. As they chugged their way up and down the village road, the three invaders were oblivious to the stares they incurred. The majority of Grodonians, returning from their fields after a long day's tiring work, were unaware of the Americans' arrival earlier in the day. They were tired and truly confused at the sight of these oddly dressed strangers *trying* to work up a sweat.

Jim, who had a tendency to tune out the world in order to complete what he considered the odious task of daily exercise, did not help matters. While Steve and Mara were used to the glazed-over look that clouded his eyes while he ran, to the villagers Jim Marlowe resembled nothing so much as old Stein on one of his crazy days. Even the Superintendent was embarrassed by his American charges as they passed him on the road home, responding with an uncomfortable smile as they greeted him in passing.

To Steve's eyes the hand-painted walls meant nothing, the only point of interest lying in what appeared to be a stylized motif of horses and dragons fading from the walls on some of the older structures. The boy thought he had seen better dragons on Saturday morning cartoons. There was also, in the Basilik, a painted bas-relief of the dying Black Horse. Carved in sandstone, it was the scene that Steve had come to dislike so much in Vavel Castle.

Despite the oddity, village opinion was not all one-sided in regard to the newcomers. As he set down another round of beer in front of Georgi and Johann, the restaurant's owner saw the running Americans through his front window and remembered the hefty tip Jim Marlowe had left the evening before.

"It means nothing to lazy asses like you, Georgi," he said with a familiar, unaggressive contempt, nodding towards the newcomers outside, "but they'll bring in money to the town."

"Not to me!" Georgi spat into his beer. "I don't need foreign money."

Johann still nursed a bandaged wrist, but managed to taunt: "That's because you've got cousins in America who send you money." His wrist ached as he hoisted his own heavy mug of beer. "Pig-stick the dog!" He winced. "I hope they go out into the forest so an 'accident' can happen."

Georgi ignored future revenges in favor of past grievance.

"Don't talk about my cousins," he protested to the world at large, "they never send enough!" He felt his last beer making gaseous rumblings in his intestines. "I know how much they make," he thought with resentment. Out loud he added: "Besides, do you think that *we'll* get anything from any foreign money?"

He saw that the restaurant owner was already smiling at American-dollar profits, so Georgi turned to the always-sympathetic, drunk visage of Johann. "Do you think that *we'll* get anything? No! Little Sturi, the little pig, will probably make them fix up the school, or something like that."

Johann knew thoughts of righteous outrage.

"No! He'll probably have the town buy him a new car! Bartan was right: when we were in school, Bartan said that Sturi—"

Georgi did not want to hear about the wisdom of Bartan: the man owed him money. "Where is that idiot brother of yours?" he demanded instead.

Johann thought heavily. He always thought heavily, but with three liters of beer in his gut these thoughts took on gargantuan proportions.

"I don't know—" he began, but then a revelation made itself known through the cloud in his brain. ". . . went hunting two weeks ago . . . probably went over the mountain again . . ." These were familiar patterns of behavior for Bartan. No one could argue with Johann's reasoning so far. ". . . got drunk . . . and crossed the border!"

Georgi—and even the restaurant owner—laughed in recognition of that probability. Bartan had crossed the border drunk several times. Each time they held him for a few weeks, shaved him, made him work, then sent him back.

"Or maybe he found 'the Jewel' up in the mountains," Johann giggled to himself. Once started, he could not stop thinking so abruptly like others did.

But the restaurant owner was horrified at the turn Johann's thoughts had taken. "He wouldn't touch the witch's daughter!" he scolded Johann, blessing himself with the sign of the cross as a second instinct.

"Why not?" Johann's thoughts were running full speed now. "She's not gold!" He smiled at Georgi conspiratorially. "But she is a 'piece,' yes? Blind little piece!"

Georgi laughed appreciatively, and Johann prepared to unleash another bolt of blasphemous witticism. But his

thoughts had grown heavy again. He drank the remaining
half-liter of beer in his mug and ordered another instead.

"Who were those guys, Dad?" Steve asked, his head
bent effortlessly to the floor.

"Coupla jerks," Jim replied. His head, too, was bent to
the polished wooden floor. Not effortlessly, though. The
backs of his legs cried in silent protest at the stretching exercise. He would have to limber up and strengthen those
legs a lot more if he intended to do any serious trekking
through the mountains on this job. He was having trouble
seeing the second hand on his watch, so he silently
counted two minutes.

"What's a jerk?" Steve bounced up from the floor and
onto the thick-mattressed bed with the ease of a spring.

"What?" Jim grappled for the right place in his count:
had he been down four or five counts of twenty?

"A jerk!"

Jim gave up and straightened out. "Those guys," he
puffed. "Those guys we keep seeing in the window are
jerks!" It had only been four counts. Jim bent down to
start again.

"Dad, what about this?"

"I can't see!"

"Then stop exercising."

"No."

Steve felt more than a little offended at his father's attitude. He looked over at Mara, curled up in a ball next to
the door.

"Mara," he called. She raised her head. Steve's hurt sen-
sibilities were confirmed: the wolf-dog would pay attention to him upon demand, why wouldn't grown-ups? With
six-year-old forbearance, he picked up the picture he had
recently drawn, slid down to the floor, and did a wall-
leaning headstand to face his father nose-to-nose. He
shoved the picture in Jim's face.

"How do you like this?"

Jim was not going to lose his count for the world.

"Very good," he said absently.

Steve brought his legs down and slid into a 180-degree leg split.

"Am I exercising?" he asked with curiosity.

"Uhhhh," Jim sighed in bitter jealousy.

"Do you like exercising?"

"No—I am in pain."

"So let's watch TV."

"No TV here."

"Then let's go home."

Jim smiled: God had given him *some* revenge on the child's suppleness. He began a series of alternate-toe touches. "Have to earn my paycheck first," he shot out before beginning the up-down grind.

"How?"

"By—signing—all the—test—OKs."

"So sign 'em and let's go home." Steve had no patience for this kind of environment. If there was no TV, there was no reason for a six-year-old to exist.

Jim gratefully counted out the end of his repetitions before grabbing up his son and holding him out at arm's length.

"Can't do that—it's *my* name on the dotted line. I've got to at least check out the obvious points." He threw the boy in a gentle arc over to bounce on the overstuffed mattress. "Get under the covers, it's cold."

And it was. The moment his body-warming exercises had ended, Jim felt the chill of the mountain air creeping into his bones. He barely finished a brief basin-only washup before he was shivering. With the stuttering step of the cold bed-goer, he skipped across the wooden floor and climbed under the down comforter next to Steve. Jim knew that fifty percent of his chill came from the lingering effects of jet lag, but he decided to skip any nighttime reading anyway. He reached up to turn off the bedside lamp.

Although he could not see the bottom half of the door, Jim clearly heard the scratching sound that came from that direction.

"No," he said aloud with a tone of terse command.

The scratching sound persisted.

"No, Mara." Jim made his command specific.

The gentle sound of claw against wood continued in rhythmic repetition: *scratch-scratch-scratch*, pause, *scratch-scratch-scratch*, pause, *scratch-scratch-*

"All right, Mara, go out! Get out!" Jim threw off his side of the comforter and stalked over to the wooden door. There the wolf-dog stood in primeval patience, her Kabuki-mask face blandly specific about what she expected from her human. Accordingly, Jim flung open the door.

"Go out! Wander the night! Stalk the wild beast! Beg cookies from unsuspecting farmers' wives!"

Mara left without comment.

"Only—don't come back until morning! . . . And don't get hit by cars!"

Jim shut the door and hurried back to squirrel under the comforter, muttering: "What am I saying: there *are* no cars here. No, the Superintendent said *he* has one—but he could be making that up, I don't think it runs." He turned out the lamp.

It felt good to warm up under a down comforter. It had been *freezing* when Jim opened the door, if not literally, then close enough for his vulnerable blood to come figuratively close to turning into ice in his very veins. Sleep was a warm darkness crowding into his consciousness, a welcome—

"Dad?"

The darkness needed only a few minutes more. "Yes?"

"How come—"

"Steve—shut up!"

Not too much damage to the sleepiness nerves, sweet dreams could shortly—

"Dad . . ."

"Steve, I said—"

"I like you."

"—OK."

The little boy curled into a warm comfortable ball next to his father.

"Like plus like makes love."

"Uh-huh. Go to sleep."

The boy yawned gloriously. "O—kay."

Jim felt his nerve endings deaden. "Go to sleep, son,"
he cautioned sleepily.

You can swim in some kinds of sleep.

Scratch-scratch-scratch.

Steve jumped up brightly.

"Dad! It's Mara!"

"Aarrghh!"

CHAPTER 8

Doc

The flashbulb was blinding, but Frank Brown liked the feel of public attention. His smile grew wider and he turned his head to face another bank of photographers. They obligingly sent their bursts of candlepower into his face. The world momentarily became a motley pattern of black dots and blue sea.

The MERCO yacht rolled gently in its mooring. The thirty-odd press and business representatives had shifted their mass too far to the port side. Brown laughed and beckoned them closer.

"C'mon, fellas, I don't want you so dazzled by my star today that you go and drown yourselves." The crowd laughed appropriately and shuffled closer to the captain's table set up on the deck. Brown leaned into the microphone. It was time to wind down the speechmaking.

"Now, despite the fact that we conducted some pretty serious business here today"—*very* serious business if it could draw all of the major business media—"I would like to announce the most important order of the day, especially for the press: dinner is served! Please join in!"

There would be no more flashbulb popping now, Brown knew, as the ravenous hordes made their way to the generous layout that had sat there temptingly for the past half hour. Besides, they all had their typed-up press releases, photo setups, and fifteen-second sound bites. No one would be wanting to talk to Frank Brown in depth about this latest bit of maneuvering by the maverick head of MERCO Industries.

In fact, Brown was more than a little pleased with himself. True, the deal *was* leveraged on the tight side. But Frank Brown had always played the longer odds. Not the longest, just a bit more risky than the prudent would abide by.

"Frank—today was brilliant!"

Brown turned his attention from the briefcase he was closing to the two vice-presidents who had just come up behind him, Tony Meerson and Sid Strang. Meerson was the younger of the two, the forty-year-old whiz kid Brown had brought up from the R&D ranks two years earlier. Strang was pushing sixty, cautious: Sid was going no further with his career and he wanted it to last as long as it could. It was Tony Meerson who offered the awestruck compliments. It was Sid Strang who leaned into Brown and spoke in a low voice.

"You play it close to the vest, Frank. I don't even think the Board of Directors knew what you were doing."

Brown smiled at the "friendly" accusation. He was safe now, the deal successfully consummated. "They didn't," he laughed.

"They didn't—?" Tony Meerson's face took on an incredulous ogle. R&D people are lousy at business strategy, Strang thought quietly in the back of his mind. He turned the corners of his lips up, reassuring the idiot whiz kid. To Brown he turned the same expression, giving a bland twist to his words:

"I won't put you on the spot by asking if you seriously meant that, Frank."

"Don't worry, Sid: I wouldn't have put you on the spot by giving a straight answer." Brown hinted a nod of recognition to the young female reporter from the *Journal* who was passing with a food-laden plate. He would have to cultivate her. She looked right out of the regional press and ready to sink her teeth readily into a few well-timed bits of "inside disinformation." One never knew when the press would be needed.

Sid Strang was not noticing the comely young reporter. He'd stepped too close to Frank Brown's blaze of glory and he wanted to extricate himself quickly.

"Today was an unmitigated success, Frank"—he tugged at Meerson's sleeve—"and it's all yours!"

Brown laughed gently to himself as he watched Strang lead Meerson away. Sid, he thought, you never were any good at playing the boardroom game. You're a good, solid drone with a head for figures, but you couldn't bluff your way through a college penny-ante poker game. Then he promptly forgot about Sid Strang. That was always Frank Brown's strong point, to think only about the necessary.

And necessary this moment was the bright-eyed, stone-faced president of the firm MERCO had just swallowed this morning. It would be called a merger in the trade papers—no stocks had traded hands, the parent company was still nominally in charge—but the assets were now the property of MERCO. Brown had mollified the man earlier in the day; now he needed to use a bit more oil as the fact became public.

But the tall, pleasant-faced man standing beside him brought Frank Brown to a sudden (if not abrupt) halt.

"Why, Doc? Thought you were in Guatemala?"

Lawrence Westmore, Ph.D. A Doctor of Sciences. The Geological Sciences, to be exact. Doc.

Doc shrugged absently. "Finished that contract. Came back to see yours here today." He gave a slight nod to the stone-faced president and others of the losing team. "What was it? Minerals? Securities?"

"A transportation contract, Doc. We're going to have certain 'exclusivities.' "

Doc produced a deviled egg in his hand, began admiring it. "Ahh," he intoned, looking intently at the egg. Almost as a side thought he added: "Did you get out of minerals?"

Frank Brown could not resist a quick glance around: there were too damned many people close by.

"It's not for general consumption that I'm *in* minerals just right now."

"Ohhh—soloing again." Doc popped the deviled egg in its entirety into his mouth. He turned to face Frank Brown and said through muffled bites: "Then why did you forget me?"

"Because you're too close to me, Doc." There was no harm in telling Doc the truth. Frank Brown was a firm believer in telling the truth whenever possible. It avoided the problem of remembering a lie.

But Doc wanted to be difficult that day.

"Karistan is a long way away, Frank."

True, Brown thought, but the problem was *here*.

"You sign the papers and I may have federal authorities questioning a conflict of interest."

A steely light came into Doc's eyes.

"My credentials are impeccable."

"I know, Doc—and you always produce."

Doc did not like competition. He worked well on his own. He was his own competition. He set his own standards.

"You know you can rely on me."

"I know." Brown was grateful for one thing: Dr. Lawrence Westmore looked like he fit in. The suit was correct, the casual attitude masking inner steel—these were qualities that looked right in the world of Frank Browns and their MERCO deals. Brown liked Doc for those qualities. But there were some times when even Frank Brown knew that a Frank Brown—or a Lawrence Westmore—would not be appropriate.

"I just don't think I'll have to use you this time, Doc. It's a simple fact. But I'll remember . . . I'll remember."

CHAPTER 9

Into the Witch's House (1)

"What is the matter, Mr. Marlowe?"

The Superintendent's bland face masked a real concern: his American guest had been shaking his head for several hours, staring at the maps the MERCO representatives had left in Grodo the year before. It was not an encouraging sign.

Had the Superintendent known the thoughts buffeting through Jim Marlowe's mind, he would have felt even more alarmed. Jim looked at the MERCO maps with a growing sense of distress. His first reaction, when the Superintendent presented them to him, was an uninhibited snort of laughter: it had to be a joke left by the MERCO geophysicists.

"These maps are thirty years old!" he said, smiling at the antiquated data forms.

But the Superintendent had answered with a straight face.

"Almost fifty years, actually—" the Superintendent explained, and as he spoke, Jim realized with the first tinglings of alarm that the maps were not an example of MERCO humor. "They started to do a mineral survey in the 1930s, but then the War started. The Germans did a very complete survey—and they forgot us again."

Well, Jim thought, someone had not forgotten the maps entirely: these were first-rate geographer's copies of the originals. First-rate reproductions of outdated surveys.

He had spent the past three-quarters of a day tramping about the Low Mountains, trying to find a grain of useful information in the data. Maybe the MERCO survey team had found that the old maps contained all the necessary information—this couldn't have been a high-priority project, Jim tried to reason.

No, he answered himself almost immediately, the maps contained far too little information to satisfy a contemporary geological survey. He began shaking his head in disbelief from the very first attempt to coordinate the maps with his own, cursory visual review of the area.

Now, as the afternoon reached its midpoint, Jim began to worry about the true implication of the maps. For whatever reason, MERCO's survey had been screwed up. It was not Jim Marlowe's business to determine whether or not valuable minerals actually existed under the subsurface of the Grodo valley region (they most probably did, though, he could tell from the exposed rock formations). It *was* his business, however, to make certain that the environmental impact study be competent enough to pass U.S. federal standards: the name on the dotted line would be Jim Marlowe—alone. No one else would share the credit. Or the blame. Frank Brown had asked for a rubber-stamp OK on the EIS. Much as Jim Marlowe would prefer to take the money and run, he knew he had to turn in a competent report.

He turned to the Superintendent and spewed out the confession he had been hoping to avoid:

"I can't use these maps, these—other—documents: they'd laugh me right out of the EPA if I submitted them as the basis for my testings."

"The 'EPA'? It is United States police, like FBI? Or is it spy organization: CIA, KGB, James Bond?" The Superintendent stepped back from Jim, performing his own "survey" of this now potentially dangerous representative of Western political control.

Jim failed to notice the change in attitude, but felt his own sense of loathing for the federal agency.

"It's worse. 'EPA' stands for Environmental Protection Agency, which should make them the good guys—except they seem to have two major character flaws: a bureaucratic mind-set and a habit for overlooking the violations of major contributors to the party in power."

"But your MERCO is large and powerful. They should have friends in power."

"I'm sure they do. I'm sure this place could be an environmental disaster waiting to happen and MERCO would probably pull off some deal with Washington. But the *paperwork* still has to be good, don't you see? The EPA likes it to look good on paper. Lots and lots of paper."

The Superintendent smiled knowingly.

"Your Washington is not so different from our Vavel. I am always drowning in paper."

Jim looked down the mountain at the small farms and single-street simplicity of Grodo.

"You have paperwork here, too?"

"Always," the Superintendent sighed, sitting on a chair-sized boulder. "Every week they want a 'Progress of the People' Report, every month a 'Progress of the People' Summary, every three months a summary of the summary, every year a—so you know. And you know.

"I will tell you." The Superintendent leaned closer to Jim, who had found a clump of grass to rest his rear on. "When I first came back to Grodo from study in the Vavel Institute for People's Superintendents, I found out that there is not so much progress all of the time in our country. Sometimes, even, there is regrets— . . . regress— . . . going backwards. I write this in my number three, maybe number four week Progress of the People Report."

The Superintendent took off his cap, tossed it to the ground at Jim's feet. He looked down at the reclining American with a sly smile.

"You are stranger here. No one will ever listen to you or trust you too close—even though they will want your

U.S. dollars. I think anything I say to you no one else in Grodo will hear."

"I don't have anything to say just yet."

"You can gossip about me," the Superintendent said to Jim's feet. "Everybody in the village likes to hear stories about how foolish Sturi the Apparatchik has been."

Jim felt uneasy. He did not like to hear others' confidences. He had shared his own thoughts with only one other person, Steve's mother. At her death Jim Marlowe had begun a series of one-sided monologues with Mara, sometimes with Steve. He expected to continue conversations with the wolf-dog. As Steve grew older, Jim became increasingly fearful of laying his own fears on the boy's shoulders.

"You don't have to—" he began.

The Superintendent cut him off.

"You need to know. Just for you. You talk like you know about your Washington, but I think my Vavel is more real to me than your Washington is to you.

"It is what I told you: I write in weekly Progress of the People Report, 'There is no progress this week, only problems. We need—' and so I write, you can guess, about the road, and water, and telephone. They are sending back my report almost same day I am writing it. My District Superintendent comes to me. He is very nice. He promises to work on the problems in my report. And he tells me very sincerely not to write about those problems again. 'In Vavel,' he explains to me, 'they do not understand the problems of the villages. They will think if we do not have progress we have counter-progress. They will not send help to villages that complain. They will find new superintendents who can make progress, not problems.' Then he gave to me important advice: tell *him* the problems, but do not write them on paper.

"Well, Mr. Marlowe, which is more honest? Every week, every month, every three months, every year I tell my District Superintendent about our problems—and I am becoming a great writer of fiction. I practice every week, every month, every three months, every year."

Jim tasted the bitter juice from a stem of long grass he had stuck in his mouth.

"Yeah, ah, I've been lucky enough not to have to write much fiction, Mr. Superintendent."

"You may call me Sturi—except in public, of course."

"Of course."

"I am not asking you to write fiction, Mr. Marl—'Jim' is OK?—Jim, write what is necessary. But remember: if your MERCO comes to our valley, there will be a new road, and telephones, and maybe a, a . . . much better life."

Jim rose to his feet. Despite the day's warmth, the mountain soil carried a perpetual dampness that had seeped into his tailbone.

"Things will change," he said.

"We are slowly creeping backwards, Jim. Things will change anyway."

Jim looked down at the Nazi-era maps.

"I'm going to have to update the maps at the very least."

"Is that hard?"

Jim thought for a moment, then realized:

"No, not really. Not for the summary job I'm going to do." Then, as always, the difficulties began intruding. "But I'll need someone who can do technical drafting." He bent a dubious eyebrow towards the surrounding vista. "What are the chances of my finding anyone within the next twenty miles?"

The Superintendent did not have to think hard to come up with a name—it was the concept that was difficult to embrace.

"It is really necessary?"

Jim immediately sensed some hope.

"Just somebody who can make it look good—I'll tell them what to do."

"N-no . . ."

"You have someone, Sturi?"

The Superintendent realized the inevitable.

"She can do it: she used to teach in the Technical Institute, before . . . she returned here. She—"

* * *

The Superintendent refused to go with Jim to the house. He waited instead near the edge of the forest, with Steve and Mara.

"She was very good," he had explained to Jim. "My brother studied under her. He did not come back here."

"Can you get her to help?" Jim asked, sensing the Superintendent's reluctant endorsement of his nominee.

"I do not think she will refuse *you*. Me, she will not talk to—and I do not want to talk to her."

When she heard the heavy knocking on the wooden door, Alta had expected to find another peasant—unusual at this late hour, the sun nearly set, for the male peasants were particularly afraid of her—or her alternate expectation had been to find someone unpleasant, like the Superintendent or the priest.

She was surprised, then, to find an American identifying himself as a "Jim Marlowe" and attempting to speak an abominable version of French. (Someone had told him that she had lived in Paris?) With a quick reassurance that she spoke English, Alta invited the Mr. Marlowe into her house, where she soon found herself surveying her own table—which the visitor had covered with old-style maps and geological documents. She recognized the work to be done and vaguely listened to the American's proposition, ". . . we would need to set a groundwork and develop a comfortable working approach—I'm not certain how they run those procedures in Europe—but the Superintendent assures me that this is well within your realm of experience." Jim looked up at the handsome woman with a tentative smile of professional camaraderie.

Alta laughed.

"Did the Superintendent also tell you why we are not talking?"

"No." Jim had hoped to avoid the topic.

But Alta appeared relaxed on the subject.

"Little Sturi is, you know, the most educated man in the village"—her English was a husky-voiced caress of elongated syllables—"but he has only a one-year technical school education. Even my daughter has a better education than he—because I have taught her! I think he has many complexes about this."

Jim's self-interest was aroused: perhaps arrangements could be made for Steve.

"You have a daughter?"

"Yes."

He needed to know more about Alta's personality before he could entrust his son to her care.

"Then why did you come back here?"

Alta did not like personal questions, but she had met enough Americans in Paris to know that it was their idle form of social amenity.

"This is where I was born. I have lived in other places."

"I figured that out—"

Alta cut him off: "I came back here many years ago."

The light tapping on the wooden door provided an escape: Alta very clearly had intended to stem further inquiry. Still, she dreaded who would be at the door. She did not want to be embarrassed by a peasant woman fawning and begging for her future just now, in front of the American.

"Excuse me."

She swept over to the door, expecting to be brusque. She found a young American boy and a wolf standing there instead.

Steve, with his usual lack of courtesy, did not bother to introduce himself, calling past the surprised figure of Alta with annoyance:

"Dad! The Superintendent sent me to find out if everything is OK!"

"Um, Steve!" Jim stepped over to the door. Looking out, he saw the Superintendent standing a hundred meters down the road. At the sight of Jim appearing in the doorway, the Superintendent nodded, gave a half-wave, then turned and walked away towards the village.

Jim looked at Alta with discomfort.

"I left my son with the Superintendent: I see he really *doesn't* want to come here. I apologize."

Alta left the doorway and returned to the map-strewn table.

"It is better—for him and for me."

Jim thought of a conspiratorial question to ease the situation:

"Tell me," he smiled, "does he really have a car?"

Alta did not bother to raise her eyes from the table.

"I will do my enemy this honor: I will not tell you."

Steve plowed past Jim and into the center of the house. He surveyed the space with a general's eye.

"This place is better than ours," he pronounced, "it has food."

Alta turned to look closer at the boy—and at the "wolf" that had followed him into her house. She saw now that it was not a pureblood.

Jim, too, turned a half-step into the house, closing the door behind him, commenting sarcastically on his son's blunt manners.

"My son, the international diplomat—ow!"

The opening door had whacked him from behind, a nice solid crack on the back. Jewel was standing in the doorway. She realized immediately what she had done and addressed the room in general.

"I'm sorry. Mother usually leaves the door open when—"

Her sentence remained uncompleted, cut off by a full-bodied crash into Jim, who was standing to what he thought was aside.

"Ooooff!"

"I—I'm sorry."

"Excuse me."

"Aaach!"

Gradually Jim became aware that the young lady with the heavy step and pointed stick was blind. His apologies took on a more insistent tone. Hers took on a more aggressive tone: Jewel did not like being deferred to. Both continued to collide with one another as Jim's efforts to help kept putting him in Jewel's way.

"I'll go this way—"

"What way is that?"

"Well, then, I'll step over here—"

"Don't change—"

"Oooch!"

"Sorry."

Steve thought the girl was being stupid, like girls always were.

"Dad, why does she keep knocking into you?"

Jewel, thinking the same thing (albeit with an anti-male slant), grabbed Jim by both shoulders and spoke in a firm, sardonically accented voice:

"Don't move."

Jim started to step out of her way again. Her reprimand was immediate:

"A-ah! Don't move! ... Pretend you are a piece of furniture: I know where you are now. And ..." She edged confidently past Jim. "When I get to the table—which should be *here*—" It was. "Now you can move."

Jewel sat down in one of the heavy wooden chairs triumphantly.

"How was my accent?" she demanded.

Jim was unready for the abrupt change of subject.

"Your what?"

Steve was not affected.

"You talk like a foreigner—and you better stop pushing my dad around!"

An awkward silence ensued, broken by Alta finally saying:

"This is my daughter, Jewel."

Jim stepped over to the table and put his hand in the young woman's.

"My name is Jim Marlowe. You heard the loud one, my son, Steve. There is also a half-wolf with us who will sell her soul for a piece of cheese. Her name is Mara and she's lying somewhere under the table near your feet."

Jewel turned her head to the direction she had last heard Alta speak.

"Mother, was my accent that bad?"

"You will have to ask Mr. Marlowe."

"Jim," he corrected.

"Yes—Jim?" The doubt in Jewel's voice was real, Jim could hear it clearly. He would not take away her imagined accomplishment.

"It was . . . very good. Right out of Brooklyn—they all have accents there." Steve didn't know what his father was talking about.

Another awkward pause.

". . . well, we—"

"Are we gonna eat supper here?" Steve demanded. "It smells OK."

The long shadows cast by the house stretched down to the main street of the village. The Superintendent was uncomfortably aware of that fact as he stepped through the shadows and into the Village Committee Meeting Hall. He had abandoned his American charges to the witch.

No, she was *not* a witch, Sturi reproached himself. She preyed upon the superstitions of the villagers, true, but Alta was an educated woman, educated in skills that the American needed. And the village now needed, if the MERCO promise of progress was to be realized. It would be awkward, he knew, dealing with the woman, but he would have to accept that fact.

From his window the Superintendent could see up the mountain as the sun set behind the witch's—*Alta's*—house. Elsewhere in the Low Mountains other shadows lengthened and conquered lakes and streams. The Table Rocks fell easy prey to the night, their always-dark mazes lost in a deeper obscurity. In the village glowing lights began to sprinkle throughout the windows. Superintendent Sturi would note in his weekly Progress of the People Report (as he had twelve times before) that Grodo now enjoyed electricity in 43 percent of the buildings that housed people. The animal shelters fared better: there was electricity in 60 percent of the barns.

CHAPTER 10

Into the Witch's House (2)

Horrible, medieval chants coursed through the mountain air, entering in vague, terrifying rhythms the peasant dwellings that stood above the village on the mountainside, emanating from the stark, moonlit silhouette of the witch's house. The rhythms seemed to repeat themselves, overlap, continue forever. The melody—if such a devil's chant could be said to possess a melody—was too faint to make out. But it was clear that the words were in the devil's own tongue, constantly changing, unknown syllables from an underworld land.

Within the witch's house, the entire ritual was obvious to the wide-eyed mask of the young boy forced to sit and witness. The witch's daughter had taken the lead from the beginning:

"Frère Jacques, Frère Jacques, dormez-vous, dormez-vous—"

Immediately the boy's father, to the son's horror, jumped in with his own croaking:

"Are you sleeping, are you sleeping, Brother John, Brother John—"

Then the witch herself added her deep, husky voice—in German!

To the boy's discomfit, the witch's daughter switched to Spanish!

His father sang now in Latin!

And the witch in Portuguese!

This was, Steve thought, the ultimate: to listen to two adults (and a teenage girl who should know better) try to be "entertaining." Why couldn't they just let him remain locked in his own, comfortable self-pity? The song petered out raggedly as such rounds always do. His father's voice boomed out:

"See, Steve, you get six channels—better than television, huh?"

"Do it again," the boy demanded, his thirst for entertainment unquenched.

"No," Jim replied with bemused finality.

"Why not?"

"Because it is boring to sing it over again every time your little demanding heart desires."

Steve sat back in his chair and sulked.

"I don't like you!" he cried with all the authority his pint-sized voice could summon.

"I like you," Alta's voice caressed his emotions. "You have clear eyes."

She had been paying close attention to both the boy and his father all evening. They were relaxed in the particular American way that was often considered boorish by Europeans—or refreshing to those, like Alta, who were constantly aware of the pretensions that had evolved in their own societies. And, of course, there was the other reason: their eyes *were* clear. Alta had avoided looking in either's eyes for hours, intending to keep the relationship with the American professional, a relaxation for herself from the constant awareness of death. But then the child had demanded dinner—Alta could not deny that she had food available, the smells were obvious—and Jewel had invited the strangers to join them. Jewel. It was her invitation. She had warmed to the voices, had begun the animated conversation that led to their first singsongy attempt to entertain the boy. And Alta could act her warmth—she had done so for her entire life in order to survive. Only later, somewhere in the middle of a song, did the act relax into something of a reality.

Something of a reality. It could never be more. No, never. Someday, Alta knew, she would look into their eyes and see their deaths. That was a given, a fact. She would not allow herself to ever become truly involved with anyone. "You have clear eyes," she had said—for now. Alta abruptly walked over to the door and opened it.

"I will be back, very soon."

She stepped out into the darkness and the door closed behind her immediately.

The abruptness of Alta's departure left a gap of uneasiness in the room. Jim, unsure of what else to say, turned to Jewel with the obvious:

" 'You have clear eyes,' she said. Does that mean we are naïve Americans?"

"No, that—" Jewel was uncomfortable with lying, but she did not want to spoil the evening. "It—just means she can be comfortable with you for a while."

Jim began gathering up his documents: it was time to leave anyway.

"I hope so. I'm going to need her help in updating these maps."

The boy could see his father hazily through the flickering of a candle on the table. The girl was easier to see: the candlelight danced in her eyes, not in front of her face.

"Oh, she's very good, I think," Jewel said. "She used to spend a lot of many times working on things like that. Some of the people were not so very nice, but I guess that is how it is with anything, yes?"

The boy began kicking his feet rhythmically against a table leg.

Jim looked askance at his documents, thinking over what Jewel had just said.

"Not so nice mapmakers? . . . I guess s—Steve! You want to bug off?"

The boy had no problem voicing his opinion.

"This is boring!"

"Talking with beautiful ladies is never boring." Jim honored Jewel with an unseen bow. "Sorry, had to sneak that in." His attitude towards his son was less gracious. "Why don't you take Mara outside for a few minutes? You-know-why."

"Why-ay?" the boy whined coyly.

"Fountain time. Scoot!"

Steve was wise enough to the ways of his father—as well as the necessities of dog ownership—to refrain from further discussion on the matter. He was glad for the diversion, actually, since the conversation between Jewel and his father threatened to continue along business lines.

"You are going to redo all the maps?" Jewel asked.

"No: I'm just going to walk over some of the major areas, do a few soil tests, update the specifics of the maps—you know, things change a lot in thirty, forty years."

Outside of the house, the heavy door closed off all inside sounds once the boy and wolf-dog had moved a few steps away. There was a chill in the air, although the thick fur of Mara was not penetrated and the high-speed metabolism of the young boy made him impervious to its effects. Steve expected Mara to pad away from him immediately and make her prerequisite wolf rounds before attending to bodily functions. Instead she stayed next to the boy. Her eyes quickly widening in adjustment to the near-perfect, moonlight-bright darkness of the mountain night, Mara found her attention caught by the "sense" of a figure moving away from the house. Her senses detected a human footstep. A moment later the boy's inferior senses also brought the movement to his attention. The dim figure was moving through the shadows of the nearby trees. In a moment it would be clearly defined by the moonlight as it stepped into a clearing.

The moonlight disappeared. The boy looked up to see several clouds crossing the white circle, cutting its light down to a pale silhouette. Then they drifted past and the renewed brilliance caused Steve to blink his eyes.

The dim figure was clear now: Alta. Stepping out from

the shadows of the trees, leaving the house receding behind her, she moved to the road's edge. The village was
laid out below her. That was what she had gone out in the
night to look at.

Steve could see Alta without difficulty, although he was
inadvertently in darkness now, lost within a shadow of the
house cast by the moon. He saw her head bent down, facing the village in the valley below. Then she abruptly
turned her head away. Almost as if in pain, Alta pressed
her fingers to her eyes, closing them, holding her face up
to the moonlight.

The boy turned his head away, too: he did not want to
see adults in private moments. Through a window, he
could see Jewel and Jim at the table. He could not hear
them, but clearly Jewel was asking some casual question.

"Do they have the caves on your maps?"

Steve saw his father look bewildered, reaching into his
knapsack to draw out a map from the documents he had
just put away.

"The caves?"

"Most of them are on top of the mountain."

Jim hastily scanned the map—there were no caves!—
only:

"Oh . . . You mean the 'Table Rocks'—I think that's
how they translate."

Jewel was becoming put out by Jim's doubting tone, a
tone bordering on the patronizing. "There are the Table
Rocks, yes," she said with her own twinge of patron-to-
peasant obviousness, "but some of them are caves. Small
ones."

Neither one noticed Alta enter from the rear of the
house. She did not particularly want to call attention to
herself. Alta observed their easy banter with an ache of
jealousy.

Jim's doubts were growing into a minor alarm.

"But those—'caves'—would be on *top* of the mountain?"

Despite her satisfaction at being superior to the American, Jewel began to feel a little uneasy: the man was making too much of this.

"Not all of the caves are to be on top . . ." she corrected herself, "and I guess not all of them are to be called small, either."

Alta gave a start at this. She stepped into the doorway of her room. She did not want to stop this conversation too early.

Jim looked closely at the map: there were no caves.

He turned his professional attention to the girl.

"Did you explore these caves?"

"No—but I know where they are. I know where everything is on the mountain—better than anyone else."

"But there are *big* ones?"

Jewel did not need to think long.

"There is at least one big cave—I did not walk very far into it—but there was a rush of air coming from it—" She smiled at the memory. "A rush of air as if from another world."

Jim was not impressed. "Very poetic," he said curtly. It probably was an adolescent fantasy trip, after all.

Jewel could hear the dismissal in his voice.

"It was hot air," she said sharply, "and it wasn't summer."

As Alta stood in the dark recess of her room, her eyes widened at the information.

Jim's reaction was more emphatic.

"Oh, hell!" he spat out, slapping the map down on the table.

Jewel was disappointed by the reaction.

"It is no help to you, yes?"

Jim leaned back in his chair, relaxed again. There was no use in taking out his frustrations on strangers.

"No, your information is a lot of help, but a pain in the ass: if you're right, then this valley can have anything from a honeycomb of rivers under the surface to a sulfur springs. Did that hot air smell bad?"

"It was years ago—I don't remember."

Steve opened the front door to let Mara in. Boy and wolf-dog saw Jim grab his head and groan.

"Aarrgghh!"

"What's the matter, Dad?"

Jim looked over at the boy. "Bring your son," Frank Brown had said, "and the dog. Have a vacation." Yeah!

"It looks like I'm really going to have to *work* to earn my paycheck, Steve: first the stupid maps, and now this ... these ... Tomorrow, son, we go cave-hunting."

Alta emerged from her room and stepped up to the table.

"Jewel can help."

Jim, trying to demur delicately, was only able to utter an awkward "Uhhh."

Jewel did not need more to goad her anger.

"I *do* know these paths better than anyone else! If you want to spend weeks searching out every hole in the ground ...!"

"She looks better than you, too, Dad!" the boy piped in.

Jim leaned back in his chair even further than he had been leaning before. Its angle was precarious now. He let it rock there a moment before easing it back to a solid four-legged position. What the hell.

"Is that the bottom line, Steve: she looks good?" He turned to Jewel. "You want to come with us as a sex object?"

"She can also transcribe your notes into notations for me to use." Alta's words were crisp, precise.

Jim was not ready for it. "Really—?"

He turned his head, looking back and forth among the three.

"I *do* have hands, *comprenez-vous*?" Jewel threw in.

Jim thought for a moment, then asked decisively:

"Do you remember the large cave, where it is?"

"No—but we will find it."

Jim stood and swept up Steve into his arms.

"OK! Tomorrow we start mapping out the caves. Good night, ladies. I will see you early in the morning." Without further waste of time, Jim held the front door open for

Mara and, after the wolf-dog had exited, followed her out into the darkness, his son still in his arms.

Alta ran her fingers through Jewel's hair. The girl was not used to so much conversation with strangers. Jewel was slightly agitated, although she would not admit it. Alta's touch calmed her. They talked of small, everyday things for a few moments as they prepared the house before going to bed. Sometime during the conversation Alta asked with offhanded indifference:

"You never mentioned the large cave before?"

Jewel could not see her mother's intense stare as she answered with equal nonchalance:

"No, I didn't—it did not mean anything before."

CHAPTER 11

Discovering a Memory

The Table Rocks stood in the morning sun as they had for centuries: a deceptive flat plain of stone that appeared to be crisscrossed by an irregular pattern of cracks. The crystalline mountain light gleamed from the hard surfaces, presenting an illusion of even more solidity. The stony "tabletop" stretched out for hundreds of meters. On this day only a boy and a dog stood within sight, two small shapes in the middle of the barren flats. They were staring down at a crack.

It was not the first crack Steve and Mara had examined this morning. A mere half meter wide, even the young boy could easily step over it. But he preferred to look down the crack—down the six-meter drop to where his father and Jewel walked along a wide passageway that would have done justice to a cathedral aisle. That was the beautiful deception of the Table Rocks: they were not a flat slab of rock at the top of a mountain, but the "roof" covering a maze of passages and chambers carved into the stone by millennia of erosive elements. Wind, rain, and snow had all made their marks on the Table Rocks. In some chambers men had cut out *their* contributions to the elemental architecture. There was evidence of occasional habitation, greater evidence of neglect. Partisans had retreated to the Table Rocks on occasion—but that had been rare: it would have been a trap if the Nazis had cut off the few entrances to the maze. It was better to avoid traps. Jewel had led Jim into the first passage without hesitation.

"Through here!" she had cried, disappearing around a tight corner outgrowth of rock.

"Just give me a few minutes to adjust my eyes," Jim had called back to the darkness, then bumped into the girl as he rounded the corner and found himself in a shaft of sunlight once again. Jewel was standing before a gaping hole. "Is this one of the caves?"

"No, but down a few steps, behind a rock, we will find a cave." She stepped away from Jim confidently and disappeared into another hollow of deep shadow.

"Behind a rock," Jim muttered, following. "It's *all* rock!"

Steve and Mara watched from above, curious small gods witness to the explorations of modern science.

Jewel's surefooted step was matched by Jim's hesitant shuffle. The girl walked with her wooden staff tapping a beat on the hard ground, her free hand held gracefully at an angle in front of her face. The man groped slightly with his hands, his eyes blinking rapidly to adjust them to the alternate striations of extreme shadow coupled with bright light.

"How did you know a cave was here?"

Jewel was no longer afraid to reveal her weaknesses: she had proved to the American hours ago her skill in maneuvering about the mountain. "I found it by accident. Everything is by accident. And then I remember—that's all."

"Weren't you afraid to go in—of the unknown?"

Jewel had to laugh. "If I were afraid of the unknown I would never leave my house! ... Here it is—" She laid her hand upon a large growth of quartz that protruded at her head level. "You have to squeeze behind and—"

"Wait a minute," Jim had interrupted, then called out: "Steve! You still up there?"

"Yeah!" the boy had answered.

"You want to come exploring a cave with us?"

"No." Steve had passed up the opportunity at the first cave. He had found a better object to hold his interest. A small rock. A very clear and beautiful small rock. Away from the Table Rocks, in the cities—or even as close as in the village of Grodo—experts would have called it a gem-stone.

The morning had continued like that: boy and wolf-dog above, man and girl below. Jewel led Jim to several caves. Most of them were very small. Jim did not bother to make more than a brief mental note of those. But two of the caves worried him. One was long, a shallow tunnel running under the surface for perhaps half a kilometer. The second cave was deep, not so deep that they could not reach the bottom, but at that bottom was running water. Jim examined the walls of these caves intently.

As they climbed out of the running-water cave, Jim sat down on a convenient stone, yawning.

"Oohhh! How many was . . . oh, seven. I need to record 'em."

Watching from above, Steve felt the chill of boredom creep into his bones: he had sat too many hours watching his father "record."

"C'mon, Mara," he commanded dully, leading the wolf-dog away. They would continue their explorations while his father worked. Steve knew enough to stay within earshot—he and Jim had worked this out long before—but the top plateau of the Table Rocks afforded a wide latitude of opportunities within that boundary.

The morning was nearly over. In the passage, Jim became aware of a hot, dusty feeling coming into the air.

"Do you need me to make notes?" Jewel asked.

Jim considered a moment. It would be diplomatic to let her help, but—

"No, these notes *I'll* make first. But—do you remember where that large cave is now?"

"Vaguely. It is in a different section. Do you mind if I walk around a bit while you make your notes? I have to count the paths for myself."

Jim could not help feeling concerned at this proposal.

"No, go ahead. Do you want to take Steve along, to hel—"

Jewel cut him off.

"No. Alone."

"Be careful."

"You should hope so: *I* know the way out from here, you don't."

"I could find my way out!" Jim protested with wounded pride.

Jewel smiled as she disappeared down the passage: she enjoyed showing up the sighted. "Ta-ra-ta-ta!" she called out, her voice echoing the feminine sarcasm. "In how many hours?"

"I could!" Jim yelled to the empty passage.

"Don't worry, I will come back for you!" laughed the responding echo.

Numbers.

Footsteps.

97-98-99-100-101. There would be a cave—there was. Continue.

333-334-335 . . .

Tunnels crossed with shafts of light, recognizable to Jewel by the sudden moments of intense light across her face. Or touching her shoulder. She liked the feeling. She was beginning to remember with more than her brain. Her entire body was beginning to "see."

"Did the air from the cave smell bad?" the American— Jim—had asked last night. Jewel was angry at herself that she had not remembered, that she *could not* remember. What was the use of a sense of smell if it did not let her "see"? She had wasted a sense, taken it for granted! That was . . . too much . . . like them! Like everyone else in the village, or Paris, or anywhere, with their sight and arrogant ignorance of their other senses! Jewel did not like feeling angry—she certainly never felt self-pity—but she could not accept the patronizing pity others thrust upon her. Well, she had proved to the American—to Jim, that's what he wanted to be called—she had proved her point. His son was unimpressed by her ability in the mountains, but the boy did not count. The boy and his animal were not deferential to her blindness, either, so she did not need to impress them. She liked Steve. She would show him a treat in a day or two, a place where his father would not need to go, but where Jewel had always found delight. And the wolf-dog. Mara. Jewel understood Mara. For a few brief minutes the night before, Mara had slid her huge head under Jewel's hand, allowed the human to grasp deeply into the thick fur and feel the power running through the muscles underneath. Power and danger. People in the village—in all of Karistan, for that matter—had terrible stories about wolves and other things of power. Theirs was a world where they were weak and always at the mercy of the powerful. The Russians had been different: they felt at one with the powerful, dangerous bear. Now the Americans came and they, too, seemed at ease with dangerous power. They ran together, power and danger. In an animal like Mara, a wolf-dog, even though Jewel could not see, she knew that there was a sight of beauty.

She smelled the horse before she heard it, heard its gentle breathing before she touched it, touched its flank with not unexpected surprise. She had stepped out of the Table Rocks and was in the small clearing that appeared briefly before the tree line began. Jewel was not afraid.

"Hello?" she called, not loudly but in a strong voice.

She was answered by the voice that had spoken when last she encountered the horse.

"Ride with me . . . Ride."

Jewel held the horse's head in her hands, feeling its muscles quite strongly beneath her grasp. Her answer was simple, without question.

"Why . . . yes, of course. I had wanted to."

The White Horse began to pace forward, as if led.

"There is a fallen log here."

Jewel stepped onto the fallen log, then easily onto the horse's back.

"I had wanted to see you . . ." It was a whisper, as clear

to her ears as the wind rustling through the trees. "Hold onto the horse's mane."

Jewel buried her hands deeply into the White Horse's long mane.

"If you keep your head low, I will tell you what we pass."

Jewel did not want to bend, not with another hand guiding, not with a chance to walk with power. "May I feel tall for a moment instead?"

"It will always be your choice."

Carefully at first, the White Horse began walking along a well-beaten path through the trees. Jewel held her head rigidly high. The White Horse sidestepped a number of low-slung branches, but her face was still brushed, some of the branches stinging. She allowed her neck to relax, bending her head to the touch of the leaves, side, down, side. But she rode high.

A break in the tree line. A treeless valley below. The White Horse stopped. His eyes saw something that was not there. Then he broke into a gallop!

The ride was fast and varied: down the valley, up the other side—splashing through the center of a stream, the water flying about—up a mountainside—stopping a moment at the top—then a leap!

The White Horse knew where he was heading, straight across the plains, past the ruins of the ancient castle. He ran his flank closely by the walls of the ruined building. Some walls were still intact. He could fly over them, but not with the girl on his back, not yet, not this first time in so many centuries. At whirlwind speed he charged down between the high walls, through the arched gateway, the wooden doors not even rotted memories on the hinges any longer.

"Bend low *now*!" the whispered voice commanded, and as Jewel obeyed, the White Horse circled and circled within the courtyard of ancient stones, his long body tilted at an impossible angle to the ground, his strange eyes glowing with excitement. It was here, the White Horse knew, *here*. *It* would not have rotted with the centuries, someone would have kept it alive. It was—

A small wooden shrine tucked in a corner of the courtyard, seen only at a glance. The White Horse did not slow his stride.

The wind played across Jewel's face, across her imagination.

She knew that they were leaving the ruined building when the horse's hooves no longer clattered across the echoing stones. They ran swiftly across the plain now, galloping to leave the broken walls receding in the distance.

Despite the breath-catching pace of the White Horse, Jewel cried out to her companion:

"Did you like it in there? Was that your favorite place we rode in?"

"They are just memories now."

The White Horse pulled up, turning to face the ruined castle across the plain, leaving the sun to shine clearly in Jewel's face.

"There were fewer people then, the stones were new—"

The road was a churning fog of dust rising to the knees. Row upon row of horses' legs cantered toward the castle. That was the view he always remembered: hooves on ground, legs crossing like the blades of scissors. The soldiers walked behind the mounted legions, their leggings of leather. Treading dully behind the knights on horseback encased in clanking metal skin. The song of the church bells reached out across the plain, past the approaching army, into the mountain where he could hear them, too. His mate would be drawn down from their mountain safehold then, beckoned to join the procession towards the walls, eyes half-shut to avoid detection. She would roll in the dust to dull her black coat before stepping in line with the pack animal train. The White Horse would do the same, joining the line next to his bewitched mate, lowering their heads together like tired beasts. Her ears twitched with excitement—was she drawn by the beauty, or the threat of exposure?—while he kept his senses alert, his eyes concentrated upon the dirt-filthed legs of the stewards in front of them on the line.

He saw, too, the clean legs of the lords and their ladies as they stepped across the new stone streets of the castle, to join the throng of peasants, all trampling over the hard-packed dirt streets of the surrounding town grown up out-side the walls. Young and old, joined by the soldiers and knights, all to turn towards the Monastery and cross them-selves solemnly.

The procession was headed by monks from the Order of St. Mikail, each carrying a censor smoking with incense. They were followed by the lay brothers, who bore the huge portrait of the blessed Archangel upon his fallen prey writhing at his horse's feet. Man-Horse-Dragon. The peo-ple in the square began singing spontaneously.

He would always see a hand clutching a gold coin, throwing it into the air toward the portrait . . .

And he would always remember that, eventually, there would be an armed hand grasping the handle of a sword, catching it in midair.

He was there, and he could remember, the Knights of the Order stretched out in their long assault line, proceed-ing across the plain, increasing their speed.

But then they became something new, a line of light cavalry, men no longer sheathed in metal, their banners crackling through the air like wings beating, crossing the plain at a gallop, their lances thrust forward—

To become something new again: still on horseback, with small wooden sticks that spouted smoke and made pathetic cracking sounds, dangerous, killing, cracking sounds—until they ran into an opposing line: there men were once again sheathed in metal, huge moving boxes of metal that spewed forth large bursts of smoke and angry explosions of death, their broken crossed insignia tearing through the cavalry lines with disastrous precision . . .

He could remember the dark silhouette of the Dragon filling the sky, bright flame enveloping the view of him, watching the men below.

He could see the face of the girl now, lit by the fiery sunlight.

Steve and Mara sat on their ledge, staring at the temptation of the faraway ruins. Jewel was out there, standing next to a horse. Steve could hear the story she was being told clearly, as clearly as the wind in the trees:

". . . just memories now. One or two would go out to be heroes. Some would be, others would not. The others would wait—and watch."

The voice paused in its storytelling. Steve saw the distant, miniature figure of Jewel mount the tiny horse, then saw horse and rider turn away from the ruins and begin a slow walk towards the Table Rocks. Mara could smell an unfamiliar, faint scent carried on the wind.

"Later," the voice continued with dismissal, "they would send them out by the hundreds—but there were never hundreds of heroes, only sacrifices. Heroes are always alone."

CHAPTER 12

A Choice of Greys

"No!"

Alta's hand continued the stroke of the pencil until the line reached its appropriate reference point, then stopped. She raised her eyes from the temporary drafting board she had set up in a corner of the room and looked over at her table. There the American hovered above the various drafts she had already prepared for him, the uncomprehending Superintendent sitting blank-faced across the table.

"No!" Jim cried again. Alta returned to her drafting: the words were not for her. She placed her measuring instruments on the old map and realigned them for a new marking. This map—and the others she had already prepared—were overlaid with several new additions. This one referenced iron deposits. On another she had drawn in an underground river. On yet another, the caves Jewel had shown the agitated geologist. The caves. No markings yet for the whereabouts of the large one. There was time. None of these maps were finished; the American's survey was only a week old.

"This isn't close to accurate! Look!"

Alta raised her eyes again to see Little Sturi wiggle uncomfortably in his chair as the American thrust a handful of documents under his nose.

"I am sorry," he whispered sotto voce, "I thought she knew how to do—"

"Alta *knows* what she is doing," Jim said sharply. "It's the originals. They're crap!"

"But they say . . . the originals . . ."

Alta did not look up from her drafting to interrupt: "It says exactly nothing, Mr. Superintendent."

The Superintendent stiffened. He had not wanted to come into the charlatan witch's house. Now that he was here, he would not be insulted by her insolence.

"These are the figures Mr. Marlowe's company gave us!"

Jim plopped into a chair and shoved the documents in front of him over to one side.

"No, these are old documents, probably picked up from the government."

"*These* are the documents your company gave us, Mr. Marlowe." Sturi had faced a hundred government inspectors over the years. He would not allow a solitary American to cow him. Not when he was in the right this time. Not to blame. Not this time.

But Jim was not interested in cowing the Superintendent.

"*My* company gave you these?"

"Yes."

"But they're based on information that's thirty years old! Older!"

"Well, the earth does not change, Mr. Marlowe." Sturi could not understand why the American was so concerned with the *age* of the documents.

Suddenly Jim had jumped to his feet and was hurrying around the table, thrusting still another of the maps under the Superintendent's nose, protesting: "No, no—they couldn't just ignore these—look!"

Sturi knew that he could look all night and into the following day and that he would still not recognize the importance of a single squiggle on the map. This did not disturb him. He had reviewed many a government directive with the same lack of comprehension, then gone on to explain it to the village collective leaders. This time was no exception. Insistence was the key. The Superintendent looked seriously at the map for a medium-length moment—too long to be curt, too short to admit real interest—then he rose from his seat and began to shuffle all of the documents spread out on the table into a neat pile. He spoke calmly and with authority, his words punctuated only by the occasional muffled humming coming from the witch in her corner.

"*These* documents and maps are what your company gave us, Mr. Marlowe. MERCO Industries had their men here for two months. They did their tests—on their own. They brought in these maps themselves—maybe they came from the central government in Vavel, maybe not, I do not know—but *these* are what they *gave* our government, and they gave me to give to you!"

"—to give to me, who gives them to you—to complete the traditional circle of socialist progressive responsibility in Karistan, where the rallying cry is: '*No*body is responsible!'" Alta's sarcastic laugh snapped across the room, stinging the Superintendent with its impudence.

It was lost on Jim, though. He stood in the middle of the room rubbing his face, his conflicting thoughts leaving no room to hear. Abruptly he turned and walked out through the front door. "Excuse me, I'll be back," he said to neither one in particular as he stepped into the darkness, absently leaving the door hanging open behind him.

He walked rapidly across the small yard in front of the house to the road's edge, stopping there with a quick movement. To any casual observer, the American was clearly agitated, making sudden gestures such as pulling his hands in and out of his pants pockets, picking up a half dozen rocks and throwing them sidearm at a tree. Completing that round of poorly aimed missile projections, Jim grabbed up another stone from the ground, tossed it up to eye level, then snatched it from the air there.

"Pretty good, Dad!" The boy's voice sounded duly impressed.

Jim turned to find Steve and Jewel standing nearby, at least one of them watching him. Mara was curled up at Jewel's feet, eyes closed.

Jim was in no mood to be applauded.

"Skunk! What are you doing up?"

"He wouldn't sleep," Jewel explained, "so I admitted failure and was bringing him here."

Jim's response was a feeble groan.

"Uhmmmm . . . Steve, do you like new computer games?"

"Uh-huh," the boy yawned.

"Blast it!"

"What is the matter?" Jewel asked. She should not have asked, she knew, for she did not know them well enough to be personal. But the father and son had been so easily open during the past week that she had fallen in with their familiarity.

Her concern was wasted on Jim, who began speaking aloud to himself in angry tones:

"I am *not* supposed to get involved with these things! I should just take the money—and run. But noooo!" He turned away from Jewel and walked halfway across the road, then stopped.

"Steve, do you really like those new toys and things?"

"Sure."

Jim made a gagging sound of disgust in the back of his throat, reversed directions, and returned to the house.

"*Gaaa!*" he croaked to the night, before realizing that the Superintendent and Alta were standing near the open doorway, watching him. Much more quietly he addressed his next comments to the Superintendent.

"I . . . don't . . . really care whose fault it is just now: I have to find out what the mining plans call for. I think the surface here is too fragile. Can you drive me to Vavel?"

The Superintendent had not expected a request for action.

"I . . ."

"You *do* have a car?" Jim demanded.

"Y-yes! I do!"

"Good. Then tomorrow morning." Jim stepped into the house and turned his attention to Alta: he had had no time for further conversation with the Superintendent. Karistan traditions be damned, they both had their immediate responsibilities. "Can I leave Steve and Mara here, and—This is a big request . . ."

"Go on." Alta nodded, bemused by the sudden, *living* activity in her house. "The boy is no problem. What is the rest?"

Jim rushed over to the table and separated out a handful of the documents.

"Can you work directly with Jewel? I need the maps updated even more."

Alta stepped over to the table, ran her finger over the maps set aside for her—one of them was dotted with the indications of underground passages that she had drafted in during the past week.

"Did you find the large cavern Jewel mentioned?" She did not raise her eyes from the map.

Jim was preoccupied with other thoughts.

"No—no, we didn't . . . I'm sorry, what?" He impulsively remembered an important point for the next day's trip.

"Superintendent, what time in the morn—"

The Superintendent was no longer in the house.

Puzzled, Jim stepped over to the doorway: he could see the Superintendent hurrying down the road towards the village.

"What time do we leave in the morning!?" Jim shouted.

"It will be ready!" the Superintendent called back, still scuttling away. "It will be ready!"

Jim turned back to Alta.

"What's he talking about?"

Alta placed a map carefully on her drafting board.

"He will probably spend the night cleaning his car and trying to make certain that it will run—so that you can have a car tomorrow. You are very lucky."

"Lucky?"

Alta sat down at the drafting board and began to pin down the map.

"He could have decided to simply take no position and let you go to Vavel on your own. That is the usual form of Karistan government."

Jim looked out the doorway again: the departing Superintendent was almost invisible in the dark night.

CHAPTER 13

Passage

The road from Grodo to Vavel had never been completed:
the village was a side trip from one place to another; there
had been no urgent need to divert government funds from
the construction of state monuments to the building of
roads for farmers. Fifty kilometers away, however, there
was a paved road—or so the Superintendent informed Jim
Marlowe as they bounced along the rutted track leading to
that engineering wonder. The Superintendent was proud of
Karistan this morning, proud of the small, battered, but
shining state automobile he was driving. The car was polished to a glowing sheen, a brilliance rapidly being dulled
by the dust clouds it was churning up. Superintendent
Sturi was aware of the several jealous looks his vehicle
provoked among the villagers as he steered past their
houses. In the 1950s, he thought with satisfaction, they
knew how to make springs and shock absorbers for auto-
mobiles. Although the American Mr. Marlowe appeared to
be somewhat motion sick, the Superintendent felt a small
thrill at the jolting ride as they sped through the valley,
past the ruined castle of the next valley, and out of the ju-
risdiction of the Superintendent of Grodo. He was going to
Vavel—on official business! He was proud.

"I asked about the large cavern: did you find it?"
Alta was seated at her drafting board, the map of under-

ground passages pinned down before her. Jewel stood behind her, in the middle of the room, trying to find the
walking stick she had left by the doorway the night before.
It was not there.

"No ... no, we did not," she answered. "He was not
looking for it only. Steve, do you have my stick?"

"Yes." Steve and Mara were on the floor together, the
boy lost in another world, playing with the stick.

"He wants to know about it now," Alta said with a pre-
tense of disinterest. "You will tell me if you find it."

Jewel reached down and snatched the walking stick
from the boy's hands. "All right."

With even more offhanded lack of interest, Alta asked:
"Was there anything else you found for him that you
had not told me of before?"

Jewel gave the question a moment's half-thought.

"No ... no."

"You could have told her about the horse," said Steve
moments later. He and Jewel had just left the road and
were entering the forest. The house was still in sight.

"Horse?"

"You didn't tell your mom about the horse yesterday,
like she asked."

Mara trailed behind Jewel and Steve. The wolf-dog
stopped in mid-stride when she heard the door to the house
open. She looked back towards the sound to see Alta
emerge, then follow them.

Alta could hear Jewel's voice through the distant clear
mountain air:

"No, I did not tell her ..."

Jewel stopped walking for a moment.

"My mother ... knows many things other people do
not ... There must be *some* secrets in the world."

The boy had already forgotten his question and had
forged on ahead. He sat on a rotting log, waiting for the
girl to catch up.

"Do you like being blind?" he asked.

Jewel was not put off by the boy's bluntness.

"No."

"How does it feel?" They were together again. Though the boy walked slightly ahead, it was clear that Jewel was deciding the directions.

"It does not feel like anything," she answered.

"Doesn't it bother you? I mean, you're pretty clumsy, y'know."

Jewel tapped Steve on the top of his head.

"Does it bother you being little?"

Steve pulled away with annoyance.

"But someday I'm gonna grow up!" he said defiantly.

More to herself than to the boy, Jewel agreed:

"That's right: someday you will grow up."

They were walking up a steep incline now.

"You gonna stop being blind someday?" Steve puffed. Beside him the wolf-dog padded with ease, unhindered by the hillside.

"No."

"Oh. Sorry." It was a matter-of-fact statement.

"No problem."

"Does it bother you, though?"

Jewel stopped walking and squatted down to Steve's level.

"You asked that before. And listen: I don't know any other way of being me, so it doesn't bother me. Besides, some places I can find my way around better than you can, even if you *can* see."

Steve would not accept such a bald-faced lie.

"No, you can't!" he cried.

Jewel would not accept such six-year-old denial.

"All right," she challenged, rising to her full height, "I will make you a bet. We are near the Table Rocks, yes?"

Steve looked up the path: to his surprise they were *very* close to the Table Rocks.

"Uh-huh," he admitted grudgingly. "What's the bet?"

Jewel allowed herself to step away from the boy. She wanted the advantage.

"A race: I will make my way to the other side of the Table Rocks before you."

Steve laughed at the joke.

"You're gonna get lost!"

"No, I will not—but you cannot cheat: don't follow Mara. *You* have to lead, not follow *her* out."

"I'm a pretty smart guy," Steve protested with all the swagger a six-year-old can muster.

"Oh, yes?" Jewel asked sweetly—then disappeared into the Table Rocks!

Steve was surprised by her sudden departure: she had simply stepped behind a large boulder—and now she was gone!

"Ste-eve!" he heard her voice echo sarcastically from the hidden passage.

"Come on, Mara!" the boy shouted, happily picking up the challenge.

To the distant observation of Alta, the boy and wolf-dog seemed to dive into the Table Rocks.

-58-59-left-1-2-3-

Stone walls racing by boy and animal.

Footsteps counted, rock walls remembered.

Furious pounding of sneakered feet, the steady clicking of claws along stone passageways.

"Can you hear me, Steve?" Jewel's voice sounded near to the boy's hearing. He smiled triumphantly.

"You better watch out! Here I come!"

The smile died: he had turned into a dead end.

-81-82-right-1-2-3-4-5-right-1-2-3-

Steve looked about uncertainly—he had been here before, he knew it—but this should not have been a dead end. He climbed the wall of the passage to stick his head up through the crack: now he could see the flat "plain" of the Table Rocks. He had his direction again, but would Jewel?

"You lost yet?" he called out.

"I never am," Jewel's voice came from far ahead. "Are you?"

"I never am!" Steve cried with the defiance of a Spartan at Thermopylae, scrambling down the passage wall and resuming the race at breakneck speed.

It was a short-lived outburst. Even as Jewel moved
through the passages at a walking pace, the boy ran head-
long into dead end after dead end. A thousand small
Stonehenges cropped up before him, mazelike, while the
girl counted her footsteps, reading her memory like a road
map. They shouted defiant taunts at one another, Steve
loath to admit defeat, Jewel confident of victory, both enjoying the chase with sweaty tremblings of thrill. Again
and again Steve found himself clambering up the passage
walls to the tabletop plains in order to find his bearings,
losing ground steadily as Jewel deftly wound her way
through the labyrinth.

To the other side: Jewel broke out onto the small clearing with a small rush of excitement.

"Success!" she shouted to the wind—let the sighted boy
hear her echo, she thought in triumph.

"I will accept that," the voice complimented her with its
quiet strength.

Jewel turned with pleased surprise at the sound.

"You are here?"

The White Horse drew close to Jewel, his flank brushing against her hand.

"You have found me."

Jewel laughed breathlessly, stroking the horse's side.

"I was running from the boy," she said.

"The boy?"

"And his pet—it is half wolf."

As Jewel's fingers caressed the White Horse's side, for
a brief moment they seemed to be touching something
harder, smooth still, yet . . . unyielding. Then she was cur-
rying the stiff horsehair again.

"How old is the boy?" the voice asked.

"Not very old," the blind girl replied.

The White Horse pricked up his ears: yes, the boy's
voice could be heard distinctly through the distortion of
echoes in the passages.

"I'm gonna beat you!" the child voice cried.

"He is very brave?" The White Horse tensed his muscles, prepared to gallop away.

With mock seriousness Jewel answered:

"Oh, yes, very brave! Aren't all b—"

Her words were cut off by the appearance of Steve, bursting into the clearing, followed by Mara.

"I won! I won! I won!—"

He stopped—very openmouthed—at the sight of Jewel standing next to the huge white horse.

"No, you did not!" Jewel laughed victoriously. "You were very slow next to me!"

Steve could not have cared less about who had won. "Whose horse is that?" he cried with unconcealed admiration.

"It belongs to my friend—" Jewel stopped, suddenly embarrassed, then turned to the White Horse. "I am sorry, I have never asked your name before."

"Tuan," was the answer.

Steve forgot to breathe.

"Tuan," Jewel repeated, tasting the sound. She turned her head to where she had last heard the boy's voice. "Steve, this is my friend, Tuan—Tuan, this is Steve and his half-wolf friend, Mara."

Steve remembered to breathe again with a huge gulp of air.

"Where did you get the talking horse?" he demanded of the girl. "This is the same horse you were riding yesterday!"

The voice began to speak:

"You saw us—"

"I really liked your story," the boy interrupted. "But how does a horse talk?"

"It does not: you *hear*. Are you afraid?"

Steve looked surprised.

"Why should I be?"

The White Horse looked over at the wolf-dog. Mara was curled up comfortably on the ground, watching attentively.

"You are not afraid, are you, wolf?"

"What is all this talk about being afraid?" Jewel interrupted impatiently. "Tell me, Steve, is he a beautiful horse?"

The small boy eyed the White Horse with TV-born expertise.

"Not bad," he said, eyelids lowered to squint in appraisal. "He's big."

"Very," Jewel agreed.

"He can ride with me."

Steve stared with wonder at the White Horse in response to the unhoped-for offer. But the animal ignored the boy, directing his attention to Mara and Jewel.

"You can walk down the hill with the wolf," Jewel heard, "and the boy can come with me."

Jewel was not offended by the choice of companions.

"Would you want that, Steve?"

Mara rose and padded next to the boy. Steve thrust his fingers deeply into her fur and clenched his hand onto the thick neck. He spoke directly to the wolf-dog:

"You take Jewel home so she doesn't get lost, OK?"

Jewel laughed smugly and turned towards the Table Rocks.

"I *won't* get lost! Is your poodle coming?"

"She's not a poodle!" Steve cried.

"Woof-woof!" Jewel barked, disappearing back into the Table Rocks. "I will wait for you by the castle!"

Mara stood next to the boy for a long moment, her attention on the White Horse, then turned and padded silently after the blind girl. Steve was left alone.

"Do you really want to ride?" came the strong, whispering voice.

Steve lowered his head.

"I am a little nervous. When I'm seven I won't be."

"But you will follow me?"

"Sure."

"Then follow."

The White Horse had not yet been near the boy, and now he paced even further away, walking with a steady step towards the Table Rocks.

From her vantage point on the flat plain above the Table

Rocks, Alta saw Steve hesitantly begin to follow the White Horse. They disappeared from sight, through a passage Alta had not seen before. It was not the passage Jewel had taken. Alta smiled knowledgeably.

As they walked together, Steve grew less apprehensive. Soon he was keeping easy pace with the White Horse, who led them through a series of winding passageways—to a seeming dead end. It was a fairly large chamber—just a passage widened to twice the normal size actually—with a large boulder fallen down before the apparent dead-end wall. The White Horse hesitated only long enough to ensure that the boy was close, then stepped around the boulder. Steve followed, practically bumping into the horse's rump, and discovered the entrance to a deeper passage behind the boulder.

The White Horse led Steve through the entrance, where the boy found himself at the rather prosaic beginning of a mine shaft, dark, but well lit by torches glowing at intervals along the tunnel walls.

"Do you want to ride now?" Steve heard himself asked.

"No." He was not ready for that, but—"How do you know when it's night here?"

"I do not care when it is night—there is no time here."

Steve looked down the long, endless tunnel.

"OK," he shrugged with acceptance.

The shaft *was* endless, and the first minutes' passage seemed to take hours to Steve. The dark walls were featureless gray monotonies, interrupted only by the torches. The White Horse's hooves clattered loudly in the tunnel. The boy could not hear his own rubber-soled feet squeaking over the trampled earth.

Then the walls began to change. Carvings appeared, bas-reliefs much like those Steve had seen in Vavel, although hard to distinguish in the flickering torchlit shadows. Many of the figures were "melted," as if they had been carved in ice, exposed to the sun, then refrozen.

The shaft widened out and out. Side "roads" crossed their tunnel. Stalactites dripped down into the large cham-

bers they now began to pass, creating pillars that separated
the chambers into aisles.

The rock walls turned a hard, bleached white.

"What is it?" Steve asked at last.

"Taste."

Steve ran a finger across the nearest wall, brought it to
his mouth.

"Salt?"

"Once there were hundreds of men here: this was the
center of their world—and they traveled around their
world taking this salt to it."

"Why did they stop?"

If the White Horse heard the small boy, he did not pause
to acknowledge the question. And the boy had lost interest
in that story anyway, for now they entered a new
passageway—connecting one large chamber with another
one seen far distant. On the ground were colored objects,
the same beautiful stones Steve had found above. But
there he had found only one. Now there were many.

Not at the beginning of the passage, though. No. At
first there were only one or two gemstones. Steve picked
the first one up, putting it into his pocket. Then the
second—again into the pocket. Then there were more: annoying at first, something to be avoided—Steve tried not
to step on them. But the precious stones became thicker on
the ground, so many, finally, that Steve could not avoid
stepping on them. Soon he was shuffling his feet through
them, stepping over piles of jewels as one would pick
one's way across a sandy beach.

And then the White Horse led Steve into the grotto
itself—

The ground was ankle-deep in the fortune, the walls
dripping with gems: they clung to the boy's pants and the
horse's mane—his tail twinkled from the reflected light re-
fracted through the crystals.

The walls were covered with something else, too: huge
canvases stretched across the grotto walls, like tapestries
seen in Vavel Castle or . . . dragons' skins. One in partic-

ular: black. Deep obsidian. The White Horse turned and stopped amidst the color.

"Did you see me before?" Steve heard the words sing softly among the gems.

"No," he answered, "only the stories."

"Then I will let you see what the girl cannot."

And there, before Steve's eyes, the change began.

The White Horse began to stamp his feet anxiously, calling the boy's attention to his hooves, plunging deeply into the precious stones, hooves suddenly transformed into the white-scaled claws of the Dragon. The strange eyes of the White Horse took in the expression on the boy's face as surprise replaced all other expressions. The boy's eyes followed up the Dragon's legs, up his white-scaled chest, broad and powerful, joined at the shoulders by two huge wings—up the long, white neck to the white-scaled, reptilian, yet very "human" head: the Dragon's broad, whiskered mouth gaped open, his sharp ears shed jewels, his large, almost "Asiatic" eyes glared down at the boy.

Those Dragon eyes saw Steve's eyes widen very large— saw the boy's mouth open into a gigantic smile!

CHAPTER 14

Tai Ching

Alta did not attempt to follow the White Horse and Steve into the Table Rocks. No, she reasoned, I am too close now to risk carelessness. The boy might lead her to the Lair, but only with Jewel there could she accomplish anything. No—I can wait, Alta convinced herself, repeating the assurance over and over as she descended the mountain. I can wait.

She had waited a lifetime. Another week, another month—knowing there was an end in sight, it was now all bearable. For so many years she had thought she would simply go mad. Or kill herself. So many haunted eyes. So many death masks. Only the thought of Jewel kept her alive. Only the thought.

Such a desperate hope to pin one's fate on, Alta thought. She had reached her house. Her face reflected the beginnings of satisfaction as she brought her hand up to the door.

The door was unlocked.

It pushed open to Alta's touch before the key could be turned. As always, the door swung wide to the slightest pressure, a faint aching sound issuing from the heavy hinges. The man standing inside the door was fully revealed—but his back was to the door and, though he must have heard it open, he did not turn to face it immediately.

Adjusting her eyes to the darker light of the interior, Alta remained at the doorstep, trying to recognize the intruder. Her first thoughts held no alarm: it was probably a peasant come for a seeing, she had probably left the door unlocked in her haste to follow Jewel and Steve. But the man's clothes were Western—definitely *not* a villager's. His build indicated a slightness of frame . . . and strength.

Alta recognized the silhouette even as the man turned finally, revealing his fine-boned Asian features, breaking into a familiar smile.

"Tai Ching!?"

"Bonjour, Alta. Comment vas-tu?"

"You are dead!"

Tai Ching shrugged, his ready smile still plastered across his face. "I have been reborn. We Taoists can be reborn, you know." He spoke French with a faintly British accent, tempered by a dozen other languages and the effort of speaking precisely in any of them. His smile left no doubt that he carried with him an implication of threat. He began to walk around the room, touching various objects familiarly.

Alta stepped into the house, countering Tai Ching's ominous friendliness with her own aggressive strength.

"Why didn't you die when there was a chance?"

"Perhaps I did—" he answered in a reflective tone, his eyes and fingers concentrated upon the items he was touching. "It has been ten years since I felt alive as I do now." He brought his eyes up to look directly at the woman. "Ten years, Alta, since you left Paris with the girl. Without telling me! And after I had removed her mother . . ."

"She is mine!" Alta hissed. "Don't talk about her 'mother'!"

"*Yours* now?" Tai Ching laughed. "Ah, maternity!"

He sat down at the table and addressed his attention to a piece of fruit. He began paring it with a small stiletto, devouring its meat with delicate ferocity while Alta slammed the door and glared at him. Ten years! she thought furiously, and five years before that caring for the whelp in Paris: fifteen years of effort, of waiting, alone for so much of it . . . Alone—but not now. It would be easier now, when she would lose Jewel—she was already losing Jewel, to the Americans—Jewel was lost to her. It would be difficult alone. But not with Tai Ching. If, after ten years, he had found her . . . Resolve and tenacity were not to be found easily, trust and partnership were the makings of necessity. Alta broke into a smile.

"You *do* know when to come!"

"Of course!" Tai Ching agreed, relaxing his shoulders—but not his grip on the stiletto. With Alta one could never fully relax. "Oh, I would have liked to watch the girl from a close perspective, but looking at this picaresque setting you have chosen"—he shuddered with disgust—"I can assume that I did not miss anything."

Alta nodded in agreement.

"Does she know?" The fine-boned eyes revealed a hard intelligence.

"No," Alta shook her head, "she still does not."

Tai Ching rose and moved next to Alta, the two standing leg-to-leg in remembered contact.

"But have her powers matured?" he asked in quiet concern. "Or do we have to wait longer—another decade?"

Again Alta shook her head. It had been so long since she had been close to anyone—except the girl.

"What has she uncovered?" Tai Ching whispered.

Alta's smile was a smile of victory.

"The Dragon."

Tai Ching took her smile and made it into an even broader one of his own. "Now, *that* is quite a potent discovery!"

He stepped away from Alta, taking a deep breath, turning his back on her. He could relax now, she needed him. Needed him more than she knew at present. The air felt deeply cool and clean in his lungs.

Tai Ching's sudden dismissal left Alta hurting, understanding as well as he that she needed him, that he had never released her even when she thought him dead. Tai Ching would use her. He always had. And she needed him.

"What are the terms?" she asked with businesslike blandness.

"For the Dragon?" Tai Ching mocked absent-mindedly. "Oh, as before."

"Is that all?" Alta could not keep the bitterness from her question.

Tai Ching heard it, smiled for it. This was his Alta.

"That is never—all."

CHAPTER 15
Break

The Central Committee of the People's Republic of Karistan had spent a long decade trying to entice foreign investment in their bankrupt government. Although they had failed admirably to prove that they would not spend loans from the money-tight Western banks on such necessary expenditures as summer resorts for government administrators, there had been one major coup: the TransContinental Hotel. A consortium of Mediterranean business concerns had made the proposal: a Western-style, Class A hotel constructed along contemporary Scandinavian standards. The pot was further sweetened by the offer of 100 percent financing in return for a modest government promise of tax-free status for ten years, followed by a graduated net-profit participation up to 15 percent—without government investment of a single hard-currency note.

The TransContinental Hotel was built. True, it did not have the style and traditional lines of the hundred-year-old European Hotel across the street. But it had air-conditioning. True, it looked like a giant mirrored ice cube set down on a parking garage. But there was twenty-four-hour room service. True, there were no longer alcoves and quiet sitting rooms for the older guests. But there was a disco and—what the hell—it looked exactly like all of the other TransContinental Hotels that dotted Europe. The government of Karistan expected West German tourists to arrive in droves.

The first guests, however, were not West Germans. They were the Mediterranean investors, who reserved the entire TransContinental Hotel for a two-week series of business meetings. As Karistan customs officers smiled in greeting, the key capos of the Sicilian, Sardinian, and Corsican Mafias sat down in *their* hotel, 100 percent free from the eyes of Western law enforcement agencies. They had found the perfect middle ground. Within a month of their departure, they reserved another two weeks: their American cousins were invited for a trouble-free confab. Soon the TransContinental Hotel *had* brought in the expected influx of travelers to Vavel: the *European* Hotel was constantly booked to overflowing by Western law enforcement agents, Interpol officials, FBI, Sûreté, Scotland Yard—everyone, in fact, who needed to keep tabs on the monthly Mafia meetings across the street at the TransContinental.

It was to the TransContinental Hotel that the Superintendent drove Jim Marlowe.

"I thought there would be a telephone somewhere on the road before now!" Jim complained as he hurried out of the car.

The Superintendent scurried behind him, certain in his heart that he had come to the right place, but nervous at stepping into such a luxury palace. He ignored the parking valets rushing towards his car, leaving them wondering what to do with the wreck left sitting in their entrance drive.

"We could have had a telephone, Mr. Marlowe"—the glass entrance portals sprung open before his face, flung wide by two liveried doormen—"but the international connection—"

Jim had heard the excuses all morning. He did not wait to listen to them again, but charged up to the broad shining expanse of fake marble that was the front desk.

"I need to make an international call. Where are your telephones?"

Jim had listened to the Superintendent's explanation all

morning, but he had not paid attention to their meaning. Now he faced the true symbol of Karistan bureaucracy: The Clerk.

She was in her late twenties to mid-forties, so lacquered that it was impossible to tell what she truly looked like. There was a faint air of imperiousness in her manner: she could speak four languages poorly in addition to her own—which she also spoke poorly—and she had been trained to follow the procedures of the TransContinental Hotel System as set down by the Official Manual. She kept the Official Manual by her post at all times. She never opened her Official Manual—reading was a bore— but she found it convenient to refer to The Manual often. Quite frequently she quoted from it. Whether or not the referenced quote existed was not a matter for her concern. She ruled the front desk in a combination of masterful inefficiency coupled with a basic stupidity: she could not handle anything out of the ordinary.

"If you want to make an international telephone connection," she answered, "simply call from your room, sir. The operator will assist you." The clerk knew that Basa, the switchboard operator, was on her lunch break. But that was not information for the guests to know. It was not in the Official Manual.

"I'm not staying here," Jim replied after he had spent a few seconds deciphering the clerk's heavily accented English.

"Oh." The clerk looked over at the ill-suited Karistan official standing next to the non-guest, asking with mistrust:

"Is *he* a guest?"

The Superintendent did not hear her question: he had let his attention drift away from the front desk, his eyes following the procession of several well-dressed Westerners and their beautiful Karistan ladies across the grand foyer. He had never been aware of so many blondes in his country before.

"No, he is not a guest, either. We need to call America." The clerk smiled painfully: they were not guests.

"You will have to pay in advance," she said. "In dollars."

Jim flashed a confident smile.

"No problem," he answered, whipping out his wallet and slapping an American Express card down on the desk in front of the woman.

The clerk looked at the plastic rectangle with displeasure: if the American had given her cash dollars she could have sold them on the black market for a sizable profit, then paid off his telephone bill in local currency at one-fifth the official rate of exchange.

"I need identification," she muttered with disappointment.

"Certainly." Jim dug deeper in his wallet. "I need to call—"

"I need your passport."

"Passport?" Jim's face fell. "I—don't have it! I left it back in Grodo." He smiled familiarly: there shouldn't be a problem. "Look, it's with my stuff ten hours drive away from here. I'm with a government official—I didn't expect to be using a public phone . . ." He pulled his library card from his wallet and placed it next to the American Express card. "See, that's me—take away the beard from the photo, of course. This is good enough for a phone call, isn't it?"

"I don't know who you are," the clerk said. "The Official Manual requires a passport for identification."

"But I don't have my passport!"

"You shouldn't leave home without it."

Jim turned away from the woman, exasperated. He saw that the Superintendent had wandered across the grand foyer and was standing at the door to the hotel restaurant, where a street musician was just entering. The TransContinental Hotel encouraged street musicians in the ground-floor restaurant; they provided "local color." This particular one was a violinist, deftly collecting money from the patrons in his outstretched hat while playing his instrument. If Jim had not felt so angry he would have been impressed by the feat. The Superintendent, however, had no clerk-inspired grudge to spoil his enjoyment and looked on happily.

The Superintendent—

Jim turned back to the desk clerk with a fury.

"Can I pay a deposit?" he demanded in a tone that left no room for refusal.

"In cash dollars?" the clerk asked, then regained a measure of her standard-issue imperiousness. "Twenty-five cash dollars," she asserted.

Jim ran across the foyer and accosted the Superintendent at the restaurant door.

"I need to pay a deposit!" he panted. "Can I borrow about twenty-five dollars?"

"Twenty-five *dollars*?" the Superintendent let the words drip out of his mouth in shocked comprehension.

"That's what she wants."

"There must be a mistake. We can pay in Karistan currency, Mr. Marlowe. Wait here." The Superintendent stalked across the foyer to the front desk with the combined strength and resolve of a petty village apparatchik for the government.

He was overwhelmed by the clerk. Jim's departure had given her time to arm herself with a few self-developed regulations from the Official Manual. In this she was supported by the current ideology of Karistan communism: the TransContinental Hotel catered to the hard-currency interests of its Western owners, *not* for the service of country superintendents. From across the foyer Jim learned the Karistinian words for "How much?" as the Superintendent repeated the phrase several times, each repetition expressed with weaker urgency. Finally the Superintendent simply stood in front of the woman, staring in disbelief. Jim crossed the foyer and came up behind him.

"Well?"

The Superintendent responded by spilling the contents of his pockets onto the desk counter.

"It is very much," he muttered, both embarrassed and angry, "very . . . I think I have it, but . . . I had not planned . . . I could feed my family for a week!" He pointed the last remark towards the clerk, who gave him a vague look in response: she was busy figuring out the five-to-one black market ratio on the exchange. Whatever the little apparatchik was saying did not fit into her calculations.

The Superintendent counted out the change in his pockets with a fumbling quickness that belied his accuracy. He, like Jim, had not expected to use his hard currency for the telephone. There was to have been a brief shopping excursion at the Western-currency shop in the TransContinental Hotel—a bottle of Scotch to impress his American Mr. Marlowe—then his own contact on the black market exchange, a cousin, would have given Sturi a four-to-one rate. The crumpled dollar bills and loose quarters added up to—

"Not enough," the Superintendent admitted with defeat.

Jim regretted his haste in pushing the Superintendent to drive to Vavel in such a hurry. "And it's Saturday," he sighed. "I imagine there are no government offices open where we can use an official telephone . . .?" Jim allowed a vague hint of hope to creep into his statement.

The Superintendent did not want to disillusion Mr. Marlowe any further about Karistan—but he knew that most telephones in his country's government offices were not equipped to make international calls without a twenty-four-hour appointment. He glanced nervously about the foyer. Two dollars and twenty-five cents short. His cousin could lend him the money, but that would be another delay: they would have to meet, drink, talk about family, and eat dinner before he could ask for a loan, even such a small one. Sturi knew his cousin: the man was a weasel, but a family traditionalist. He did not think that Mr. Marlowe would have the patience to go through the rituals.

Two dollars and twenty-five cents.

Where to find . . .

The restaurant.

The Superintendent was ashamed of his idea. But was there a choice?

"Excuse me, Mr. Jim," he said, shoving the inadequate

pile of money over in the American's direction. "I will go
to get the rest for you from the restaurant."

Sturi did not wait for Jim Marlowe to respond in any
way. He did not want to be halted even for a second or he
would lose his resolve. The TransContinental Hotel was a
hard-currency establishment. The restaurant accepted only
Western money, its patrons foreigners—who liked "colorful" Karistan traditions.

He removed his cap as he approached the restaurant
door and pulled a small harmonica from his coat pocket.
The Maître d' gave only a cursory glance at his attire and
instrumentation, then nodded Sturi in: they accepted new
entertainment every few minutes during the dinner hour. "I
take twenty percent," he whispered as the musician passed
in.

Inside, the Superintendent looked about uncertainly for
a moment. Then he brought the harmonica to his lips. Almost without intention, a gentle, introductory "he-ho" sang
out. It was not even an introduction, really, more of a
rhythmic warm-up—the typical restaurant musician's
catchphrase to attract attention prior to performing a song.
The patrons at the table next to Sturi recognized their cue
immediately: two quarters were stuffed in his cap while it
hung loosely in his hand, then the patrons turned back to
their conversation, ignoring him completely.

Sturi puffed more strongly on the mouth organ, attract-
ing a wider circle of attention with his he-hoing rhythm.
Now *he* took the initiative, thrusting the cap out at table
after table. The diners looked up absently as he approached them, most of them vaguely aware of the man
playing for them. The blond Karistan women glared hard-
eyed at the intrusion on their companions' attentions, the
foreign men fumbled coins and paper money into the cap,
anxious to impress their female counterparts with their
wealth, rarely taking their eyes off the women or the food
long enough to notice the musician. The Superintendent
continued the he-ho introduction as he made the circuit of
the room, finally returning to the entrance door under the
watchful eye of the Maître d'. Sturi stopped playing in

mid-ho, made a quick bow to the patrons, then hurried out the door.

"You didn't play anything!" the Maître d' whispered furiously, grabbing at the Superintendent's arm.

Sturi pulled away and shot the Maître d' a look of "official right."

"I don't know how," he answered with authority.

The patrons commenced a confused scattering of applause in his wake.

The Superintendent hurried across the foyer as fast as he could without running, pausing at the front desk only long enough to drop his money-filled cap in front of Jim.

"Here, Mr. Jim, I will be driving around the block! Come out to the street when you are finishing your telephoning."

He hurried out the front door and pushed past the annoyed parking valets to climb into his car. The concept of tipping them for standing there looking at his vehicle was foreign to his thoughts at the moment, his major concern being whether or not the motor would start on the first try. It did. As he coasted away from the TransContinental Hotel, the Superintendent could see the front entrance in his rearview mirror: the Maître d' had just emerged, accompanied by two burly waiters, none of them smiling.

More than a little disoriented by the quick departure of the Superintendent, Jim turned back to the clerk and shoveled a handful of Western currency from the cap.

"Here. Let me make that call now."

The clerk smiled—it would be a profitable day.

"Certainly, sir. It will take some minutes to connect you through to America. Please sit down and I will call for you." The clerk looked at her wristwatch and made a small calculation: Basa, the switchboard operator, would be back from her break in a quarter hour, no need to trouble the American with that information. International calls always took a long time to connect through.

It was ten o'clock at night in the executive offices of MERCO Industries. The day's work was not close to completion. Junior execs rubbed elbows with their senior vice-presidents as they trudged continually in and out of the large conference room that had been commandeered as Frank Brown's command HQ. The man himself, many commented, still had his spacious office securely sacrosanct against the sour smell of sweat and disorder that littered the activity center. They had started the meetings at eight that morning, each VP and division head sequestered in the conference room and cut off from his own office-cum-support-base, connected only by the messenger-aide services of their junior executives. Only Frank Brown was allowed to enter and leave at will, returning to his office for whatever backup he deemed necessary, emerging fresh and newly dressed at three-hour intervals.

No one was physically constrained to the conference room, of course—but that was the genius of Frank Brown's management style: to leave and return to one's own office would be a minimum half-hour trip for his executive staff. It would "break the rhythm of progress" that Frank Brown—and the MERCO Industries he guided—so vehemently advocated for these sessions. And no one could argue with his success rate. Frank Brown's charismatic tactics had successfully thwarted two hostile take-over bids in the past decade and made an end run around a Securities and Exchange Commission investigation into a major transaction that had pulled MERCO up into the Top 100. "Beat 'em with energy and endurance and a burst of strength that leaves them licking your heels," declared Frank Brown at every Board meeting. He lived his own philosophy.

And it was a philosophy being put to the test once again, as always on the hard edge of disaster and success. Political tides and years of government benign neglect were backfiring on the big-business world in a series of tightened markets and curtailed finance sources. New rules were being written. Giants had crashed overnight.

The MERCO Industries were not immune to the new environment. As Frank Brown walked quickly from one group of execs to another, winding his way through men disheveled by the long day's set of nonstop meetings, he noted the smell of general consternation in the air. As always, Brown presented a figure strongly resistant to the others' self-doubts. While immediate subordinates slumped in shirt sleeves and loosened ties, Brown moved briskly about, still in his coat, his tie straight, the walk definitive.

"Frank, the figures on the Brazil Project don't add up?!"

Brown turned to face the small crowd huddled around the Brazil Project documentation.

"*Make* them work, Willie, make them work."

Brown turned on his heel and walked out of the conference room at that point: he did not want them to press him for specifics—hell, that's what *they* were hired for!

Two junior executives passed him, entering the conference room as Brown stepped out into the wide, deeply carpeted hall. The walls were naked, shorn of the usual generic corporate art, handsome in their mahogany strength of grain. Brown left the noise of the conference room behind as he strode several paces down the hall. Even without the public eye Frank Brown remained firmly in command. He took out his key and unlocked the door to the executive washroom. It was empty. He entered.

Inside the washroom, Brown stepped over to the sink and carefully turned the brass faucet knob until a small trickle of cold water splashed in minor cadenzas into the black marble sink. He spread his fingers beneath the small stream—they were shaking, he noticed with annoyance—wetting the tips. A moment later Brown closed his eyes and pressed the wet fingertips against his eyelids. Small drops of water coursed down his cheeks, too small to make their way past the gridwork of tiny, sun-inspired wrinkles that patterned his face, disappearing before their moisture could reach his chin.

The door opened with a suddenness too obvious to be accidental. Brown opened his eyes to see one of his senior staff standing in crumpled anxiety behind him. It was Willie, William Magroder, from the Brazil Project.

"Frank, there's a call for you—from Karistan."

* * *

Jim had spent the previous hour trying not to fall asleep from fatigue in the hotel armchair while waiting for the international call to go through. Now he was growing increasingly annoyed at the information he was receiving from Frank Brown.

"No!" he shouted loudly into the receiver, trying to overcome the limitations of the outmoded Karistan telephone system. "My analysis is *not* faulty! What do you think I—"

"I did not question *your* ability, Jim," Frank Brown said with persuasive dispassion into the cordless telephone he had taken from Willie in the hallway outside the conference room. "I was merely trying to make the point that your findings must be presented in a form that the governments will understand correctly."

"There's nothing more to understand: you go into there with a full-scale operation and half the valley will be sucked underground within ten, fifteen years." A haze of static swept over the line. Jim shouted over it: "The substructure is too weak!"

"Ten years is a long time—"

Jim interrupted: "It happened in Louisiana in the seventies—a whole lake just disappeared!"

"—we only are contracted for seven years." There was a faint hint of the Bostonian in Brown's voice. More and more he found his speech patterns returning to their university-day accents.

The desk clerk looked at the American with vague annoyance: why are all foreigners so loud? she thought. She glanced at her watch repeatedly, timing the call. The American had been shouting so loudly, and now he was talking in a slow cadence:

"Seven years?" Jim asked. "And then?"

Brown nodded to three VPs who were retreating from the conference room: without his constant presence as a catalyst, Brown knew, the day session would peter out. This call had taken too long.

"All rights revert to the local government," he answered

with a degree of displeasure certain to convey itself to Karistan. "So you see, Jim, your reports must be presented in such a way that they can be properly . . . evaluated."

Jim understood Frank Brown's displeasure clearly.

". . . You son of a bitch . . . You would do that, wouldn't you?"

Brown realized he had said too much.

"Do what, Mr. Marlowe? You seem to be very tired: just bring us the—"

"You're going to screw—"

"—*bring* us the reports and we'll—"

"I'm not going to bring you any—"

Brown did not bother to conceal his anger:

"—*we'll* rework them. *Don't* breach procedure, Mr. Marlowe. Do as you're told: hand in your reports, then step away. You have overstepped the limit of your responsibilities already."

There was no immediate answer. Brown took the opportunity to look into the conference room: it was half-empty. Only the Brazil Project group remained. They were arguing weakly, shaking their heads over the documents. Jim Marlowe's voice interrupted his observations with a quiet threat, nearly impossible to hear through the poor connection:

"I'll turn in the reports, Mr. Brown, to the two governments. See you in New York next week!"

Jim handed the receiver to the clerk, then dumped the remaining contents of the Superintendent's cap onto the front desk.

"Keep the change," he said absently, turning to leave the hotel. The desk clerk looked over at the switchboard: Basa was not paying attention, as usual. The clerk cut two minutes from the bill and retallied the cost of the call. It was a profitable day.

There was no need to stand out in the hallway any longer; the conference room was deserted, for all intents and purposes. Frank Brown walked in and sank down onto a hard-backed chair. He did not have the desire to walk back to his office. Not yet. The conference room was where he had designated the work space for this day. Frank Brown still had work to do. He dialed the number from memory. He remembered every telephone number he had ever needed to know.

"Hello?"

"Doc? This is Frank Brown. I'm going to have to terminate one of my employees. Could you go and see that he turns in his resignation properly?"

CHAPTER 16

Cycles of History

Quiet. How very, very quiet. Steve did not ordinarily think in terms of that word, but that was what the boy thought now as he looked through the dark, starry, half-moonlit sky. He tilted his head down: there was the earth, a dream, an almost shapeless "ocean" below. This was for only a second, maybe two seconds, a lifelong moment before . . .

Everything began to move at once—suddenly the ground was rushing upwards!

The earth drew closer—closer to the point of collision—and then—a swoop back up towards the stars!

Steve clung tightly to the white-scaled neck, his hand buried deep beneath the scales, practically lying along the outstretched muscles as the Dragon soared almost to the heavens.

Higher.

Higher!

A break in the clouds revealed the half-moon once again, revealed the silhouette of the Dragon—the human form toylike above the powerful wings—as it stopped for one brief moment in midflight, then dropped down again.

His wings outspread as if they were parachutes, his legs outstretched to meet the earth, the Dragon Tuan glided safely down to the wooded mountainside, his charge, Steve, still safely riding on his back.

From his broken-down cabin at the foot of the mountain, old Stein saw the Dragon once again. He felt hurriedly for the small, flat case containing his "collection": it was there, in his coat pocket. Stein hugged it for reassurance. He was not drunk—although he did like to drink—and he was not half-asleep, stepping out of the cabin to relieve himself in the middle of the night, looking up at the sky with sleep-dirtied eyes as he wet the ground between his feet. This time it was early in the evening, the sun had set only an hour before. Stein had gone out to gather firewood against the cloudy, damp night. He saw the Dragon through a break in the clouds.

Stein had seen the Dragon seven times in his lifetime. The first time was as a young man, hiding with the Resistance in the Table Rocks. Sent out to watch for Germans, it had also been a cloudy night. The other nights had been cloudy, too. Cloudy, thick nights, enough years apart to keep his hopes alive. He had told everyone about the Dragon—and everyone had bought him a drink or sent him to the doctor's clinic three villages and five valleys away. All of them said he was crazy. Harmless, but crazy. They did not believe him about the other things, either: houses that flew and trees that talked. So now he would not tell them about this new sighting of the Dragon, being ridden by a boy. Unless he needed a drink, of course.

Only the witch had ever listened to him, years ago when she returned from the West. But she was a witch, she would not buy him a drink.

Maybe the Chinaman would be at the tavern tonight? Stein smiled at the recent memory of two days before. The Chinaman.

Georgi and Johann—they never bought him a drink—had been playing dice in the tavern, rolling the spotted bones across the heavy wooden table in desultory fashion while grumbling as always. The Chinaman had entered and sat at another table across the room.

"Another foreigner!" said Georgi, spitting on the floor—and then, across the room, the Chinaman spit on the floor, too!

Johann rose to his feet, woozy with anger, but the Chinaman only smiled and remained sitting.

"I do not like foreigners, either, but"—he spread his arms apologetically—"here I am." The Chinaman rose from his seat and crossed the room towards Georgi and Johann. "I would like to apologize for my presence," he said, producing a bottle of Frenchy brandy and placing it on the table, "and, perhaps, play with you."

Georgi and Johann, of course, did not share the brandy with Stein—he remembered their piggish greed well enough. The Chinaman sat with them for an hour, losing at some turns with the dice, winning more often. In the end, he had gathered most of the locals' coins in front of him. Then he surprised the room by producing a handful of Western currency and fanning it out across the table.

"Tell me about this witch of yours . . ." He smiled with confident curiosity.

He was not disappointed: Georgi and Johann would have shared their slanders with anyone for free. For money they raked their memories and presented the Chinaman with a legion of petty horror stories. The Chinaman sat and listened, his face growing increasingly bland in its impatience as the tales continued with their pointless accusations. Stein watched, thirsty for the diminishing brandy. He was unaware of the sudden flicker of life in the Chinaman's eyes when his own name had come up in connection with his Dragon stories: how the witch had even been stupid enough to listen to crazy Stein. The stories continued, running out of steam rapidly after that. Sometime during the storytelling the brandy was finished and Stein wandered out of the tavern.

It had been noontime or a little later when the Chinaman arrived: it was now the hottest part of the afternoon. Stein found himself a comfortable patch of soft dirt in the small alley behind the tavern, his stomach crossed by the warm sunlight while his head leaned back against the shaded wall. He must have fallen asleep, he remembered that, although he also must have been looking at his collection before falling asleep, for the thin, flat case was in his hands when the Chinaman woke him up.

It frightened Stein to open his eyes and find the Chinaman's face in front of his own. Stein made a motion to leave—but the Chinaman did not move: Stein's position was too submissive, too difficult to rise from. He stayed where he was.

The Chinaman sat down on the doorstep next to Stein, aiming a forefinger at the flat, thin case.

"My collection," Stein said in his thick, retarded accent.

"Show me—please," the Chinaman had asked, producing a new bottle of Frenchy brandy—a *full* bottle—and putting it next to Stein. Stein remembered opening the collection case and showing it proudly to the Chinaman.

"Very pretty." The Chinaman ran his eyes along the three short rows of crudely pinned butterflies and moths.

Stein had always found talking difficult.

"Things fly," he said defensively.

"Of course they do," the Chinaman smiled. "Do they also change?"

Stein swallowed, surprised that someone would understand!

"Do you know?" he asked.

With elaborate innocence the Chinaman pointed to the collection.

"Butterflies change . . ." he said.

"Moths change," Stein agreed.

"Other things change," the Chinaman added.

"Horses," Stein had confided, before losing the afternoon in the Frenchy brandy.

The wolf-dog stared through the comforting flames of the small campfire, warmed by the heat, watching the sightless eyes of the blind girl as she leaned forward. The girl was reading her memories again, lost in them, and Mara could hear the clatter of the approaching hooves for a full minute before Jewel did. But, shaking her head back into the present, the girl understood their meaning instantly. She was on her feet to greet the small boy sitting

atop the huge horse long before they entered the circle of
light cast by the campfire.

"Good evening, travelers!" she called out to the dark
forest. "How was your moonlight ride?"

Tuan's eyes sparkled as he approached.

"The horse was very slow tonight, yes?"

Steve slid off the White Horse and turned back to smile
at Tuan:

"Yes!" he agreed.

Jewel laughed. "Why don't I believe you?"

Steve walked over to Jewel and took her face in his
hands, saying with six-year-old pomposity:

"Believe me."

"Oh, I do," she answered good-humoredly. "I should
believe him, Tuan?"

The Dragon's claws were stretched out into the fire.

"Yes."

Steve ran over to Mara, grabbing up a blanket that was
along the way, and leaned back against the soft body of
the wolf-dog to watch the flames.

"How do the stars look?" Jewel asked.

Steve's eyes were already feeling heavy-lidded as he
heard Tuan answer:

"Like diamonds from an ancient necklace."

Bedecked in jewels, the White Horse glided across the
forest path, flashing quickly between the trees. Riderless,
saddleless, the animal held itself as if *he* were a rider. His
progress was steady, almost silent, his hooves muffled by
the fallen leaves. That was the problem: the same fallen
leaves that masked the sound of his passage could no
longer fill the trees and cloak his escape. The calls of several hunting horns screeched through the air. The White
Horse heard dozens of horses' hooves clattering along the
rocks below.

Below the forest the entire mountain surrounding the
Table Rocks had been planted with hedges by the monks
a century earlier. Grown now to a near-solid wall, the Pursuers would be held back only until—they found the break

in the hedges and emerged: knights and their stewards armed and closing in. They sighted their prey easily.

This had been *her* doing, of course—drawn once again by the bells and the echoed song—and it had been a trap. His mate had found seclusion more and more difficult for the past cycle of human lifetimes, choosing repeatedly to shed her protection and walk among the walls, a Black Horse intent upon watching the activities of the *living*, instead of waiting, safely, with him.

And they had been found out.

Oh so clever, the Knights of the Order—the lessons they must have learned on their Crusades! Never mind that neither monster had challenged their power. Some pair of sharp eyes had uncovered their disguise, there had been a conference, the trap was laid: the bells were rung and monks sang their seductive, hypocritical songs.

The White Dragon did not feel the trap, but as always he pleaded:

"Do not go."

The Black Dragon twined her long ebony neck with his, bringing their bright, intelligent eyes level.

"It is a hundred times you have feared—and a hundred times we have returned, safe."

He would not refuse her: he, too, had become addicted to the contact, forgetting the Law of Nature and the Failure of Man. As White Horse and Black Horse, mate and mate, they left the safety of their Lair, descended the mountain, crossed the empty plain, stepped into the trap.

Oddly, for all his fears, *she* sensed the trap before the White Horse.

By then it was too late, though: the walls were in sight, then clouds of dust appeared on the flat horizons. The two "horses" were surrounded by an overwhelming army: a thousand peasants, a hundred stewards, dozens of mounted knights had joined to draw in the net.

It was an impossible battle on this open plain, and the two beasts did not try to engage in it. Their nature would not allow them to return to their true selves and flee. But the trap was not fully closed, and as horses they made their break for the mountain. Once they had broken through the line—accomplished with ease—only the mounted knights and a few stewards could follow. The plan from there was simple: the White Horse lagged behind, allowing his mate to make her escape to the Lair hidden in the Table Rocks, while he led the majority of Pursuers on a roundabout, reducing their ranks as their nonmagical mounts fell out of the chase, exhausted.

He had run them through two valleys, cutting their ranks to a quarter the original strength. Now he could make for the safety of his Lair and, if necessary, fight.

The White Horse shook his head: showers of colored gemstones fell to the ground. He turned and made for the cover of a stand of evergreens, galloping towards the Table Rocks.

The Pursuers were not able to make so quick a progress, the communication between horse and man not developed enough to allow them to weave among the trees with the ease of the White Horse. Three stewards and a knight were knocked from their mounts, one with a crushed leg, the others lucky to escape with only easily healed wounds.

The White Horse ran up to the entrance to the Table Rocks, stopped and turned to face the oncoming Pursuers. From within the Table Rocks, the Black Horse emerged to join him, her eyes glittering with excitement and—sadness? They could both see through the near-leafless forest below them: the Pursuers were making their way towards the Table Rocks.

Only one Pursuer did not join the others. This knight had traveled long and far in the Holy Lands, fought for the Honor of God and Saracen treasure, losing the first, never winning the second. Now he knelt to the ground and picked up an iron-gloved fist full of the jewels the White Horse had just shed. His eyes bright with wonder and belief, the knight looked up to see the other Pursuers pushing past him through the forest to the Table Rocks. He had what he had sought, the knight decided, let them have the glory. He was the last man to see them alive, but he was not to know it. He never returned to the Monastery of the

Order of St. Mikail, never looked back as he rode away down the mountain. There was a lord's title to be bought in his native Tuscany. His vows to the Order could stay in Karistan.

The eyes of the White Horse glistened like the precious gems falling from his sides. His front legs had already begun the change, no longer long, smooth, and hooved: they were thick, white-scaled, clawed.

He saw the Pursuers break from the tree line into the small clearing just before the Table Rocks. Their gallop came almost to a stop.

He saw the Black Horse's eyes glisten as his had, her hooves stamping on the hard ground. She was hesitating. Tuan turned his Dragon's head—

"Change!"

The small, pathetically short arrow dug deeply into her black chest.

The Black Horse reared on her hind legs, crying in agony.

"And the moon?" Jewel asked.

Tuan turned his Dragon's head to look at Steve: the boy was asleep.

"It does not matter."

Jewel felt the sadness in his voice, misread its meaning.

"I know it does not matter, at least not to me—but I should ask, shouldn't I?"

The Dragon turned his strange eyes to look at the girl.

"To see? No."

Why should anyone ask for what one does not have? he thought.

"But you could see again . . . someday."

"How?"

The Dragon's eyes formed many colors.

"At the death of something beautiful to you. There is a small miracle in every death."

Jewel considered his words.

"Then I shall never see, I suppose: nothing should die for me."

With a dismissive gesture she added:

"Besides, I don't miss it, this 'seeing.' "

"Why?" the voice whispered.

"Do you really want to know?" Jewel asked. She had given her usual response of casual defiance, the snappy answer that worked so well with the oversolicitous sighted who wanted to be reassured that their own self-indulgent pity would not have to extend beyond a minute's concern. She knew that this conversation demanded an honest answer. She had not been honest with herself on this point for years. No one had asked her to be.

"Because—" and she remembered how she had finally consoled herself years ago. "—because if I see . . . it could never be equal to what I have imagined it to be like."

Mara raised her head, suddenly alert. The Dragon's eyes lost their colors.

From the tree line, a few moments later, Georgi and Johann stumbled, arguing between themselves. Carrying rifles.

"—I don't care, Johann," Georgi slurred aggressively, "you've been drinking like a pig and you couldn' shoot a—witch's bitch!"

Georgi and Johann realized together that they had stumbled upon more than just a fellow poacher's company. Their drink-hazed survey of the scene took in the situation quickly: a blind girl, a sleeping boy, that dangerous wolf-dog—and a white horse?

"Hello?" Jewel called towards their voices. She recognized them, of course. One was the poacher Bartan's cowbrained brother. "Can we help you?"

Johann elbowed Georgi.

"It's the witch's daughter," he whispered loudly. "Blind as a witch's tit!" He giggled at his own clever wordplay.

"What do you want?" Jewel asked, speaking in the precise language of literary Karistinian.

Georgi put a hand over Johann's mouth and tried to speak on the same cultured level:

"We are hunting, madam—miss—my brother disappeared a month ago and—"

"So we'll shoot a few pheasants to make up for it!" Johann cut in, laughing in heavy jerks.

Georgi hit him a resounding thump across the back.

"Thass my brother!" he cried.

"Nobody liked him anyway!" Johann shouted back, swinging wide with his open hand at Georgi's face.

Mara slid out from under Steve, stood up with hunched shoulders, and began growling at the intruders.

Johann jerked his head angrily in her direction.

"It's the damn wolf!" he cried, raising his rifle and pulling at the trigger.

The rifle cracked—the same pathetic sound the White Horse remembered so well—and Mara was hit. She gave a short yelp and was knocked back!

Steve, half awakened by the shouts before, jumped to his feet.

"What are you doing?" Jewel screamed at the men.

"Mara!" Steve cried, running over to the fallen wolf-dog, lying at the White Horse's feet.

The White Horse reared up. Steve backed away.

"She is only wounded. Do not worry."

At the sound of the voice, Georgi and Johann looked about confusedly.

"Wha—. . . Who was that? . . . Where? . . ."

Georgi recovered first.

"There was nothing!" He shook his partner angrily, turning the man towards Jewel. "Nobody except The Witch's bitch! Yes, daughter of darkness!"

He threw down his gun and began to advance on the blind girl, a lustful glint in his drunken eyes.

The White Horse stamped his hooves.

Georgi stopped suddenly, looking down at the ground: there were several large, beautifully colored gemstones by the campfire. Johann stepped up behind him.

"Georgi!" he whispered. "They came from the horse!"

Georgi tore his attention from the precious stones to look in the direction of the White Horse.

The White Horse's legs changed to hard-scaled claws.

Georgi and Johann began to believe in God—and the Devil.

Steve kept his gaze squarely, hatefully on the two men.

Behind him, with a casual, almost dancelike elegance, the Dragon craned his long neck to tower over the boy, lean towards the two men—and change them to stone!

Steve's eyes and mouth popped open in wonder.

"Ahhh!" he whispered in ecstatic, delicious awe.

Jewel called out, worried:

"Steve! Tuan! *Vous êtes ça va*!?" she cried out, forgetting to speak a language they could understand. She held out her thick mountain walking stick, turning towards the last direction she had heard the intruders speak from.

"If they are hurt, you will die!" she said with an intensity that brooked no doubt.

"It is over, do not worry," she heard.

"What has happened to them?" Jewel demanded, her anger still hot and unsatisfied.

The Dragon's eyes sparkled with many colors.

"They have left."

CHAPTER 17

Needs

"No, yesss, yes, could be . . . no, no, no."

Alta leaned against the closed door to her bedroom, annoyance competing with boredom as she watched the American shuffle back and forth between her drafting board and table, where his idiotic Nazi maps were spread out in disarray. Tai Ching was in the bedroom behind her—was he sleeping, or listening to Jim Marlowe's stuttering chatter? Marlowe and Little Sturi had stumbled into her house hours after it had grown dark, the Superintendent's noisy car engine announcing their approach minutes before they arrived at the door. Tai Ching did not want them to know he was there. Alta did not care: they were part of her past. There was a future now. Finally, after so many years. She had no interest in the past.

Jim crumpled up document after document. "These are useless," he said by way of explanation as he dropped them to the floor. His words were for the Superintendent, who stood looking over his shoulder, looking blankly on, yawning frequently. Jim fought to overcome his own fatigue, internal agitation working to pump adrenaline into his exhausted nervous system as he went over the new reports Alta had drawn up quickly, dismissing some, keeping others. But still—

He looked across the room at Alta. "That's all?"

"That is all you gave me," she answered dully, her eyes

focused on a small mirror hung next to the door: it reflected the half-moon that had hung in the black mountain sky since sundown.

"Not enough," Jim muttered to himself. He turned to the Superintendent to elaborate:

"You understand? *I* know what has to go into the reports, but I need more facts, more data."

"Y-yes," the Superintendent agreed, stifling a yawn.

"You need more sleep, yes, Mr. Superintendent?" Alta observed sarcastically.

The Superintendent felt immediately foolish, like a schoolboy caught dozing in class. Jim came to his quick defense.

"We've been on the road sixteen hours today. He has a right to be tired."

"Of course!" Alta shrugged. "And tomorrow you will understand what Mr. Marlowe is saying better, yes?"

"I will understand," the Superintendent protested tersely.

"Of course!"

Jim could not pretend that he was unaware of their animosity, but he chose to ignore it. He appealed to Alta:

"I need your help. We—"

"She will not help," the Superintendent cut in. There was more conviction than venom in his voice, and Jim looked inquiringly at the Superintendent. He waited for Alta to contradict the statement: there was an awkward moment of silence instead.

"He is right—" Alta said at last. "I have other business now. You will have to draw your own little pictures." She went over to her drafting table and began unpinning the map secured there. "Does that make you relieved?" she said over her shoulder to the Superintendent.

But Jim refused to be the loser in the Alta-Superintendent personality clash.

"I *need* your help," he insisted.

"*That* is why she will not help you, Mr. Marlowe." It was the Superintendent's turn to be sarcastic. "When someone *needs* something she . . ." He paused, leaving the phrase uncompleted.

" 'She'—what?" Jim demanded, looking from one to the other. "What are you two up to?"

Alta did not listen to the American's complaint: her attention was involuntarily attracted to the Superintendent's eyes. An intense shudder ran through her body, and she turned her face away.

The Superintendent felt his face pale, his skin grow cold. With an effort he prevented himself from shuddering like the witch. He looked at her through bitter eyes.

"Your performance is very good," he said, tight-lipped with dignity.

Alta quietly removed the map from the drafting board and placed it on the table. She began to assemble the scattered documents on the table into neat piles: she wanted the American to leave without further incident.

Jim saw her dismissive actions, matched by the Superintendent's sudden tense formality, and cried out angrily:

"What is this crap?! What are you two talking about!?"

Alta continued to arrange the documents. The Superintendent answered stiffly:

"The 'witch's' powers see death in my eyes—at a convenient time." He reached past Alta and took his cap from the table, turning to leave the house. "I will help you, Mr. Marlowe, as much as I can."

The Superintendent fit his cap onto his head, opened the door, and left.

From within the bedroom, Tai Ching heard the door close quietly. By habit he walked silently to the bedroom door and listened for further sound: he had only heard one pair of footsteps leave the house. He could not see Jim looking at Alta: she had ordered the documents into categorical piles, laid the piles together, and was bundling them into a large folder.

"And you?" Jim said to her back.

"I have refused." She did not want to look in the American's eyes.

Behind the bedroom door, Tai Ching was pleased by her answer.

Jim angrily grabbed up his papers.

"Your timing is very good!" he spat. Controlling his rising anger, he added in hurried, measured tones: "Please bring my son home when he returns with Jewel." He left the house without waiting for an answer.

Emerging into the darkness, Jim was momentarily disoriented. Stumbling down the three stairs from the doorway, he searched unsuccessfully for the Superintendent along the road. With little concern for his own safety, Jim plowed across the small yard, clipping his arm against something soft.

"Please! Excuse me!" he heard Jewel whisper in the darkness.

Jim had been moving across the yard so fast that he was several feet past the girl when he realized what he had bumped into and turned around. His eyes had by this time become accustomed to the darkness enough for him to make out the dim outline of Jewel carrying the sleeping Steve. She was staggering, actually, the unconscious boy a dead weight in her arms.

"I—uh—excuse me," Jim stumbled with embarrassment, rushing over to take the boy from her arms. "Here! Let me—"

He felt Jewel's hand on his arm before he could fully grasp Steve.

"Oh, it's you, Jim," she said with recognition. A moment later Jim was burdened with the leaden weight of the sleeping boy. "Please: your son is very heavy," Jewel sighed with relief at the release of shucking off her load.

"I know, I'm sorry," Jim whispered.

"No problem. I'm sorry we are so late."

"I'm . . ." Jim began.

"—sorry," Jewel laughed softly.

"—yes! Sorry!" Jim found himself laughing as well. "I'm sor—No!" He stopped himself: "*Thank you*, I mean, for taking care of Steve. I'm not thinking too well," he tried to explain, "I'm tired and just . . . just angry, to be honest: I'm afraid your mother left me high and dry."

"You need her help," Jewel said. It was not a question.

"Yes. How did you know?"

Jewel found herself stepping towards the road, away from her house. Away from the two friends who would now leave, disappointed.

"It happens—always. Once, before we left Paris ..." She was tired of being a part of Alta's disappointments. "Can I help you?"

Jim was tired: from the sleeping boy in his arms, from the day's long travel, from the problems that cropped up from just trying to do his job right. "I need Alta's drafting skills," he answered.

But the idea was growing in the girl's mind, and she was not so tired as the man: her resolve would not be put off by his exhaustion.

"*You* do the drafting," Jewel said with increasing enthusiasm. "*I* will give you all the information you need: I am used to counting my steps. They are exactly sixty centimeters. I am understanding the past three days? You do not care about the minerals in the earth, you want to know about the underground passages, about where they are and how long they are: I am correct?"

"Yes!" Jim could not hold back a small, good-natured laugh at Jewel's enthusiasm.

"Do you want my help?" she demanded, her young woman's pride completely at risk.

Jim was intrigued by the offer: it was workable.

"Do I have a choice?' he said, a twinkle in his voice.

"I would put it in nicer terms than that." Jewel was pleasantly annoyed.

"You would?" Jim smiled.

Jewel walked back toward the direction of his voice, stopping when her shuffled toe met his. "I would," she teased, bringing her hand up to touch Jim's face—this was her "eye contact." She had not really "seen" Jim before this moment.

Jim shifted Steve in his arms and brought his own right hand free. He closed his eyes to let the girl "read" his face, then raised his hand up to touch her face with the same familiarity.

"Even if I had a choice, I'd want your help."

They stood there "looking" at one another for a long moment. Jewel gently stepped closer to Jim, resting her head on his shoulder, cradled weightlessly in his arm next to Steve. There was a small tear in her eye.

"I wonder how you look?" she asked quietly.

Alta could see them through the window, reflected in the small mirror hanging by the door. In one night: another death mask and—the final loss of Jewel. She did not particularly care when the arrow sliced through the air across the room and pierced the colorful heart of the hanging tapestry on the wall over her head. She already knew the details of the legend that Tai Ching would explain.

"The metal itself is nothing remarkable," he droned in French, stepping over to the tapestry and pulling the arrow from the wall, "but it must contain bronze—and it must hit the Dragon's heart."

He waited for Alta to speak. After an appropriate pause to show her disinterest, she stroked his ego.

"You seem much more 'able' than when we were in Paris, Tai Ching."

"No," he answered simply. He had noticed her distraction earlier, noticed the point of reference. Without allowing his silhouette to cross the curtains, Tai Ching walked over to the window to share in Alta's thoughts. His own obsessions intruded instead:

"But when they left me for dead, I wanted them to think they had beaten a weak man. They did not try hard enough." He fit another arrow into the crossbow he held loosely. "They should have—I told the last one that."

Alta rose suddenly and stepped next to Tai Ching.

"Have you priced the Dragon?"

"Priceless. For the teeth alone we can have millions. The eyes, the heart—Southeast Asia, China—they're open now: I can start a bidding war!"

Alta interrupted with a quiet trembling of emotion:

"They are very potent medicines, powers—you do not want to use them?"

Tai Ching considered her question: he had asked it himself many times.

"No—I have tasted the thought, but I am much happier watching people like you play with the power." He had no illusions about himself, nor about anyone. That was the key to dealing with the magic ones, Tai Ching had decided years earlier. It was the key to dealing with *anyone*.

Alta saw Jewel clearly through the crack in the curtains: the girl was talking with the American, making plans for the next day's sortie into the mountains.

"She's not blind, you know—" Alta thought it time to explain the difference to Tai Ching, a difference it had taken her ten years to learn. "But just as I can see only the darkness, she can see only the light."

"Therefore," Tai Ching smiled ruefully, drawing the correct conclusion, "*she* cannot see anything in this world, while *you* can: reality has more darkness, yes?" He crowed mildly: "I told you that at the beginning. These are my legends, not yours: your people have forgotten them. That is why I stole the child for you."

"You did not know what she would find someday!" Alta stepped away from the window.

"I could guess."

"But you could not know!" Alta said, despair filling her heart. "*I* could not know, except . . . to know . . . that it would be the thing that would bring her sight—and bring me peace."

Tai Ching looked at her incredulously. He had never imagined Alta to have desires any less philistine than his own.

"You would give up your 'sight'?" he asked, for once less self-possessed than Alta.

But Alta's admission would allow no more room for emotion. With businesslike abruptness she began moving about the room, sweeping away the drafting tools.

"I pity Jewel for having to see," she said, "but, then, it will only be for the moment before she dies—and I look forward to being blind. She will lead us to the Dragon's lair. She . . . will."

CHAPTER 18

Mapping

The next two days were probably the most confused of Jim Marlowe's life. Starting with too little sleep on the first morning, joined by the exhausted Superintendent, the blind girl, and the seemingly energy-injected Steve, Jim forced himself to lead the "team" up the Low Mountains and work the survey with specific objectives in mind. In order to make a convincing argument against the MERCO project, reason dictated, he would have to provide documented proof of his assertions: the outdated maps—partially revised by Alta—needed to be made more complete. That was impossible, Jim knew, without a many-weeks survey by a professional field team. But there were key data references that *he,* working alone, *could* indicate. Not conclusive in themselves, no, but indicative of the problems the MERCO project would initiate. Frank Brown had been right: presented in the "proper" light, the valley's substructure weaknesses would appear unaffected—especially as they showed up in the underdocumented MERCO reports. Jim could alter that perception radically by filling in the indicators of the central substructure system. Nothing conclusive—no time, tools, or personnel for that—but examples glaring enough to cause the U.S. and Karistan governments to think twice. That's what Jim was paid for—or, as Jim realized sourly, what he *had* been paid for: he entertained serious doubts that the weekly paycheck was continuing to be deposited in his account. But he had been *hired* to make an environmental impact report. That was his job. Even if Frank Brown did not like the answers. That was Jim Marlowe's job.

But God!, Jim groaned through the first day, why did it have to be with sore feet and amateurs?

Day One was almost a comic disaster. Despite Jim's agreement with Jewel that the main thrust of his work would be in mapping out the underground passages, a certain amount of soil and rock strata information had to be collected. This was easy enough on the flat surfaces: Jim took the samples, made the field analyses, then wrote down the results. Later, however, he found himself dangling by a rope on the face of a fifty-foot cliff, calling out the results of his visual strata survey to the Superintendent, painfully hauling himself back up to the top to find that Sturi was so unfamiliar with geological terminology that his notes from Jim's dictation were virtually useless. Jewel had insisted on doing the writing then and it suddenly developed into a delicate moment: should Jim insult the Superintendent by considering him so incompetent that he was replaceable by a blind girl—and could the blind girl do it?

In the end the matter was solved by calling on the Superintendent's pride: Jim used Sturi to physically help with the distance surveys, holding the measuring plumb a hundred meters away while Jim discreetly dictated the distances to Jewel.

By midafternoon, somehow, a working arrangement had fallen into place, with Sturi providing the muscle and legwork, Jewel the paraprofessional support—and even Steve contributing: he carried the paper and food supplies in his small rucksack. Before the first day was over, Jim had discovered oil and tar seeping from under the marshy ground nearby the valley's small river—and indications that Karistan, or at least this southern region, was hit by regular earth tremors that had cracked the foundations of every house older than World War II.

Day Two started slowly. Jim and the Superintendent both felt the effects of their long trip to Vavel more acutely than the day before. Away from the hearing of Steve and Jewel, the two complained of stiffened butt muscles that left them walking like old men. But midmorning found Jim loosened up, at least, and they made rapid progress in their survey: Jim wanted to concentrate on underground passages, which Jewel found for him with speedy accuracy. The previous week's slow survey had sharpened her memory.

At noon the Superintendent left the party. Despite the pressing nature of the survey, he needed to attend to the business of his district. He had brought his car this day, however, and he drove the others as close to the Table Rocks as possible, leaving them off in the middle of the forest before heading back to the village. He promised to return at sundown, saving them an hour's walk down the mountain.

The Table Rocks. All of the underground passages appeared to have some connection with the Table Rocks. As Jim sketched in the locations of the small and medium-sized passages, patterns seemed to take shape upon the map. They were seated at the same circle of rocks where Jewel had built the campfire for Steve two nights earlier when Jim first noticed the pattern.

"Y'know," he said, brushing away the rubber scrapings from a section he had just erased, "if I was an anthropologist I'd think we were uncovering a Pueblo Indian community."

But he had no thoughts beyond that quick observation, the needs of the survey dominating his attention. Jewel recalled the stepping count to three small caves nearby and Jim converted her footsteps into map scale measurements. Steve, recognizing the circle of stones they sat in, grew anxious.

"Can I go exploring for Mara, Dad?" he asked, already walking towards the Table Rocks.

"Don't go too far," Jim replied without looking up from his map. It was annoying to carry the portable drafting board into the mountains, but he needed to work fast. He mentioned to Jewel: "Where *is* Mara, anyway? She usually doesn't stay out all night."

"She was gone yesterday, too," came the gentle reprimand.

"Yesterday?" Jim raised his head suddenly. "I wasn't think—"

"Mara is with my friend Tuan," Jewel reassured him. "She was hurt by poachers. Tuan is taking care of her."

"What?!" Jim rose to his feet, scattering his drawings in the dirt. Like most men, his feeling of helplessness and concern showed itself as anger. "Stupid animal, I knew this would happen someday! Is she all right?"

"Tuan said she was. He will bring her back tonight."

Jim turned his concern to Steve, shouting to the boy:

"Steve! Don't go far away!"

In point of fact, Steve was *not* very far away: he was only at the edge of the Table Rocks, very close to the circle of stones where Jim stood. Steve looked back at his overreacting father with world-weary patience.

"I'm going into the rocks," he explained. "OK?"

He did not bother to wait for an answer: Jim had too much work to do to stop the boy, they both knew that.

But Jim's concern had not died down altogether.

"Is he safe in there?" he asked Jewel.

Jewel, too, recognized the annoying symptoms of a guilt reaction: Steve had been exploring the rocks for two weeks already; it was somewhat late for Jim to be worried.

"He is safer than in the forest," she said with measured calmness. "If he becomes lost in there, I can find him, and if he does not become lost—then there is no problem."

Jim felt a slight twinge of dubious concern at this reasoning.

"Ehh . . . I'll give him five minutes between call-ins."

Steve was already deeply inside the Table Rocks, winding his way confidently through the passageways. The lesson of his race with Jewel had not been lost on the boy and, though he did not count his steps as she did, he recognized now-familiar landmarks by sight and feel. The stone walls, blank to him only days before, now seemed to have direction signs written across each crack and outcropping. Steve turned the requisite lefts and rights without problem.

Coming finally to the small dead end where Mara lay resting in the sun next to the Dragon.

"Hi," the boy said with matter-of-fact familiarity as he went to crouch next to the wolf-dog.

"You are alone," he heard.

Steve slid over to Tuan and leaned his back against the Dragon's hard side: not as soft as Mara, but more solid—and smoother than the rock walls.

"No," he answered, "my Dad's outside with Jewel: she's helping him. I think she likes him, too, which is good."

"Why does she help?"

"'Cause my Dad's a good guy."

Steve took off his shoes and ran his feet over the deep fur of the wolf-dog.

"You gonna be all right, Mara?"

"She will be well."

"Ste-eve!" Jim's voice echoed into the chamber from a distant passage.

The Dragon's eyes swam with color.

"That is your father."

Steve was surprised. "How did you know?"

"I have heard the voice of heroes before."

Steve could not help but turn a cockeyed expression to the Dragon.

"My Dad's not a hero!"

"You are lucky: he is."

Jim's voice was louder this time, closer: "Steve!"

The Dragon flexed a muscle, pushing the boy away from his side.

"Go to him. Do not lead him here."

Steve scrambled to his feet. The wolf-dog did not.

"You bringing Mara tonight?"

"Yes."

"OK!"

The boy was gone.

The Dragon and the wolf-dog knelt alone in the chamber, hearing the voices of the humans as they met, argued over a petty point of direction, then retreated through the passageways. Tuan twisted his long neck in a graceful arc to look at Mara's eyes.

"We cannot be sad—can we? They are human: they will die before they have a chance to remember."

From far away, high above the earth, the engines of a jet airliner screamed their entrance into Karistan.

CHAPTER 19

Recruiting Tactics

The strong, driving beat of the music could be heard clearly, despite the fact that it was filtered through earphones that were firmly attached to Doc's ears. The airplane seat next to him was empty: the passenger ticketed there had long since deserted his place. Each of the remaining passengers around Doc—the old Karistinian in the seat behind, the matron with her crying baby seated in front, particularly the West German business executive in the seat across the aisle—all had quietly complained to the stewardess at one time or another since boarding the plane in Vienna.

"Why do you not tell him yourself?" she thought when first asked by the West German. She was Hungaro-Austrian herself and not fond of Germans in general. She also could hardly hear the music at first, the dulling *boom-boom-boom* from the earphones lost in the cacophony of preflight takeoff confusion and the wailing baby nearby.

Nevertheless, the stewardess turned to the earphone-wearing American and prepared to make her usual slightly-stern-but-understanding admonitions. Then Doc smiled.

"*Guten Tag,*" he said in precise, unaccented German. "Will you get me a glass of mineral water, please? Now."

Later, during the flight, the stewardess reflected on her failure to correct the passenger. Her failure, then her acquiescence to a request that had had no place in her preflight preparations. She checked the passenger list: the American controlling seats A–C in Row 7 was Westmore, *Doctor* Lawrence Westmore. He was dressed in perfect conformity to the standards of a university professor on a trip to Europe. She should have had no hesitancy in telling him to turn the volume down on his portable tape player, especially since she had by that time received the clandestine complaints of all the affected passengers near him. She put down the passenger list and prepared to correct his behavior.

Then she remembered his eyes.

She let him play his music.

Doc felt the music pound through his body, in perfect sync with his racing heartbeat. Since Frank Brown had called him, providing an anonymous manila envelope with details and cash for expenses within the hour, Doc's body had sung with adrenaline. He had avoided alcohol the entire eighteen hours of the trip in order to keep that edge. This was what he lived for. The Edge. He had arranged a six-hour stopover in Vienna, slept for four of those hours at an airport hotel, and still kept The Edge. His eyes reflected The Edge.

Doc's entire posture reflected The Edge. As he exited the airplane, moving in sync with the music and his heartbeat—totally out of step with the airport—Doc walked deliberately past the dozens of people in the small Vavel Airport lobby. He did not need to push through the hugging relatives and baggage-heavy foreigners that clogged his way: The Edge, the slightly "wild" look to his body movements, had people stepping aside willingly.

Except for the woman who blocked his way.

She stood near the only exit to the lobby. As Doc approached, clearly intending to leave the airport, she stepped forward and stood strongly in his path. Doc walked directly up to the woman. She did not flinch from the effects of his attention, as the clerks and attendants had along the journey. Doc stopped a bare two inches from her face. He could smell her clean, blond hair. The corners of his mouth broke into a thin smile of irony.

"The police?" he asked with blatant innocence.

Doc looked down from her face to survey his roadblock completely: the woman was very attractive. Her "business" dress was cut low, with the same provocation as that showing in her eyes. She laughed with sarcastic familiarity back at the American:

"Of course, Doc!"

They sauntered out of the airport together, to the fast-rhythmed beat of the music still pouring through Doc's earphones. As they stepped out the exit door, the woman tossed her head provocatively and gave the security guard standing there an overly familiar and totally unwarranted pat on the cheek.

The woman, Karita, had arranged a room at the Trans-Continental Hotel, of course. Doc had entered the country wearing only the travel clothes on his back and carrying Frank Brown's manila envelope. An hour after arriving in Karistan, he emerged from the Western-currency stores at the TransContinental fully outfitted. It was afternoon. The Edge was still sharp. Doc went to work immediately.

"You were lucky I was here, Doc," Karita said, sitting across from him at a small table in the bar she had found for him. It was a bar that could best be described as grey and dingy. A Vavel workers' bar in the declining socialist state of Karistan. For "Vavelkos": workers without enough work. It was perfect.

"I would have made my own luck if you weren't," Doc answered, looking around objectively. The bar was full, although not crowded, filled with characters who looked like they would eat nails for breakfast—if half of them still had their front teeth to eat the nails with. Doc knew that he and Karita were clearly out of place, particularly in the attire category. There were other "peculiarities" as well: after ordering a bottle of brandy, Doc had produced two shot glasses from a pocket. He made a small show of polishing them and replacing the cheap, bar-provided "snifters" with the heavy shot glasses. He then filled each shot glass to the brim: Karita sipped at hers delicately, Doc pointedly ignored his. The other patrons watched the two out of the corners of their eyes.

Doc put that consideration on hold—he had other business to attend to first.

"Here," he said, shoving a TransContinental envelope across to Karita. "Keep this." It was addressed to a bookstore in New York.

"What is it?"

"Just a letter—with nothing in it *you* can use," he smiled. Doc understood Karita very well. "Mail it if I don't take it back from you in three days . . . You talked about luck: that's how I make my luck." He reached across and lifted up the unsealed flap on the envelope. "Read it," he nodded, pushing up the letter inside with his thumb.

Karita read slowly—English was not her first language—but with complete comprehension. Her eyes began to widen.

"Who is this?" she asked at last, refolding the letter and returning it carefully to the TransContinental envelope.

Doc smiled, slowly and carefully: The Edge had full possession of him now, but his actions were still thought out, considered.

"My current employer."

"But—you'd send out evidence to the authorities on *everyone* you have worked for?"

"Already set up." Doc closed his eyes, visualizing the distribution network he had arranged. "If I don't call in every month, it all goes!"

Karita could not comprehend Doc's gamble with such high-stakes employers. Still, this was Doc's risk, not hers. "Why?" she demanded, without passion, but professionally curious. "Do they know you're doing this to them?"

"No." Doc shrugged in the Italian manner. "It's not to cover my back, if that's what you think . . . Let's just say: I want to be remembered." With a sudden shift of interests, he brought his eyes into focus with hers.

"I'll need guns."

"I have an Uzi here," Karita answered, starting to reach down into the large handbag lying at her feet.

Doc shook his head, putting a pause to her movement. "I'll need a lot."

"How many?"

Doc began smiling again, a reckless smile this time, a smile for show.

"I don't know: let's find out."

And with that, Doc grabbed up his long-neglected shot of brandy, downed the burning liquid in one swallow, then tossed the shot glass up in the air and caught it high above his head. This trick elicited a small scattering of sarcastic applause from the rough onlookers, who were no longer trying to hide their interest in the strangers. One or two even laughed appreciatively—until Doc responded by spitting out the alcohol with overacted distaste.

"Isn't there anything but frog urine in this country?" he complained loudly.

There was a moment of restless inaction as those who could speak English translated to their co-drinkers. Even without the translation, everyone had understood the aggressive tone. Even without the aggressive tone, everyone had felt insulted by having someone so different in their midst.

But now "national pride" dominated the onlookers' thoughts. Despite the fact that their descriptions of the state-manufactured brandy ran to more scatological observations than Doc's had, no true-minded Vavelko would let a foreigner make such an insult. After a few seconds' muttered consultation, one of the onlookers called out in hoarse English:

"You can always drink your own piss!"

A roar of laughter greeted this previously translated retort—cut off when Doc singled the Speaker out from the crowd and directed his next comment to him personally.

"I might as well: it's better than paying for yours!" He tossed a coin at the man's feet.

Translation was no longer necessary at this point. The Speaker jerked his head rapidly from side to side, looking to his two nearest countrymen for support. The half-drunken trio shoved themselves away from the bar counter, heading for Doc's table.

Doc stood up with swift, visible strength of purpose to face their approach, the suddenness of which caused the three Vavelkos to stop immediately. In a low voice, he directed his next words to their ears only.

"Not here."

But, of course, his words were overheard, and as the three looked around uncertainly, a translation was provided. Almost at the same moment, another patron kicked open the back door: it led into a dingy alley. Doc's three aggressors looked sullenly at him, then turned and headed out the door. Doc followed. Karita sipped calmly at her brandy, made a face at the taste, then produced a pint bottle of Scotch from her large handbag.

The Vavelkos found themselves forming an impromptu semicircle around the back door. This was not unusual: each of them had had experience in this sort of encounter before. The Speaker immediately sought, and found, a conveniently sized board standing against the wall near the door. One colleague was wrapping his belt around his right fist. The third did not need boards or belts: he was a sometime bricklayer, his hammer-like hands callused to the point of insensitivity. They waited for the American with grisly anticipation. None of them were particularly upset about the uneven odds in their favor.

Doc, for his part, stepped out of the bar without hesitation, observed the developing situation carefully, then closed the door behind him. He did not smile, but his eyes glinted with a certain "light" in them that was unsettling to the Vavelkos. He stepped into the middle of their semicircle, facing the board-wielding Speaker, with Belt Fist and Hammer Hands on each side.

The four men stood still for a moment, the Vavelkos uncertain, Doc unhurried. Finally, the Speaker smacked his board ominously onto the ground.

"Maybe you want to drink your own piss now?"

There was not a breath of time between word and response: Doc slammed Belt Fist in the chest with his right elbow, bounced over to the opposite side, plunging his right fist deep into Hammer Hands' solar plexus, then shot his left hand straight forward to smash into the Speaker's jaw!

Three seconds later the back door burst open into the bar from the force of the Speaker's body being thrown against it. The door sprang to its furthest extension, hit the wall, then ricocheted back to slam closed. A moment later Karita looked up from her smooth Scotch to see Hammer Hands carom into the room. Once again the back door arced back, gouged a chunk of plaster from the wall, then began to spring shut. Belt Fist's head met the heavy wood first as he hurtled into the bar. No more bodies flew through the door to keep it open and it began to swing shut with force.

It was stopped in mid-swing by Doc's outstretched hand.

Karita enjoyed the sight with calm amusement—barring the moment when she had to waste half a shot of good Scotch on the face of a drooling local who was leaning over her shoulder: everyone in the bar had stopped talking to look at the doorway. They saw only Doc's hand for a moment, holding the door. Then Doc appeared, swinging the door open with controlled force, filling the doorway. After a quick survey of the opposition, he strode into the center of the room.

With casual cruelty, Doc stepped over the fallen body of Hammer Hands to give the still-unconscious Belt Fist a shove with his foot. At this outrage, a black-capped drinker rushed from the crowd, swinging his fists wildy. Doc took him out with a punch to the stomach. Still another Vavelko began to attack angrily, jumping onto the bar counter and leaping at Doc—who simply stepped back and let the man hit the ground with a thud, knocking him out disinterestedly with a bottle taken from a nearby table.

Now the entire room was on its feet, the angry Vavelkos crowding together densely in an ever-tightening circle around the foreigner. They had learned from the earlier examples: no one made any foolish, single-handed attempts to bring down the stranger. This was a group press, impossible to fight alone, about to break into open attack—when a burst of machine-gun fire stopped everyone dead in their tracks!

Karita was standing by the entrance to the bar, blocking its closed door with her body—and holding the Uzi automatic pistol whose bullets had just shattered pieces of the ceiling above.

But the patrons of the bar had their attentions distracted even more by the sudden shout from the American standing in the center of their circle:

"Gentlemen!" Doc cried.

The confused Vavelkos turned to face Doc—who held in his hands, fanned out in delightful color, lots and lots of money. Lots and lots of money. A beautiful green color.

CHAPTER 20
Yin-Yang-Yang

Day Two of the survey marathon was finally near its end—barring the long walk down the mountain. It had been a long, extremely productive day, but Jim wondered whether he had been wise to send the Superintendent back to Grodo with his car. Yes, the extra three hours up in the Table Rocks had been worthwhile—the darkness was no hindrance to Jewel's cave-finding—still, Jim's muscles groaned, it *was* an hour's walk down the mountain to drop off Jewel, another twenty minutes to the village.

Jewel and Steve did not seem as tired as he was, Jim observed in hurried glances, lifting his head up from the various papers he fought hard to read in the weak campfire light. They had returned to the circle of stones near the Table Rocks where they had set up base earlier in the day. All three washed down freeze-dried foods with mountain spring water while Jim tried to tie down the loose ends of the day's research. At the moment he was attempting—with mixed success—to coordinate Jewel's measurements with some gaps on the old map he had set aside for underground passages.

". . . but I have never gone any further in." The girl stared blankly at the campfire, absently playing a finger-wrestling game with Steve as she remembered aloud. "The last tunnel I can remember is two hundred steps long—"

"Two hundred even?" Jim asked, hastily setting up the

151

arithmetic conversion of sixty centimeters times two-hundred footsteps on his pocket calculator.

"Yes," Jewel replied, "exactly two hundred steps. I was surprised, too: nothing ever works out so perfectly."

Jim stared at the answer flashed out on his calculator.

"Well, don't worry: it doesn't come out so even for me."

"It starts forty steps from the big stone at the river—do you have that already?"

Jim nodded yes—then remembered to add an affirmative grunt.

"—and it comes out on the other side of the river at the water mill."

"Food!" Steve barked, breaking off his finger-wrestling with Jewel after his twelfth consecutive loss.

Jim did not look up from his work.

"Use the magic word," he ordered, "and your arm isn't broken."

With patient annoyance, the boy replied:

"*Please* may I have more food—for Mara."

As Steve had expected, this brought Jim's nose up from out of his work, a surprised expression of disorientation crossing his features. And, indeed, Mara *was* walking into the circle of light cast by the campfire. She padded next to the boy as if she had only been gone a few minutes, curling up at his side.

"Mara!?" Jim repeated a half dozen times as the wolf-dog made her entrance. He was pleased to see her. "Well—of course she can have food. Here, Mara—" He tossed her something unidentifiable. "Your favorite: freeze-dried mystery meat!"

The wolf-dog scarfed it down in one snap.

"She likes it!" Steve cried, always delighted at the sight of Mara's large teeth snapping closed with power.

"God knows why," Jim grumbled with stylized crotchetiness.

Jewel liked the good-natured insults between the Americans. She decided to join the fun.

"I liked it, Jim."

"You couldn't see it. I liked it, too—but that's more a tribute to starvation than taste." He tossed a packet of freeze-dried meat to Steve with the comment: "If your Mother could see you eating this, I'd be shot."

"Shot!" Steve laughed, then grew serious. "Dad, I have two favors. Can I ask them?"

"Ask away."

"Is Mom really gonna come back to life someday?"

Jim did not answer at once. He was embarrassed by this type of question in front of others. He looked over at Jewel but, of course, her eyes were blank.

"That's what they say," he answered at last, seriously, but without elaboration.

Steve had thought about that often, and he needed to explain his thoughts to his father.

"Well, I like you a lot, but are we gonna see Mom when she comes back?"

"I don't think so."

"Don't worry about missing your mother, Steve," Jewel said, filling the long silence that had developed between father and son. "Mothers change: she would not be the same now anyway."

Jim looked curiously at the girl.

"That's a new one on me. Is this the radical feminist interpretation of motherhood, developing here in the metropolis of Grodo and waiting to burst upon the world?"

Jewel burst out laughing at Jim's overcomplicated reaction.

"No! I don't know what you are saying, Jim, but it is true what I said! I remember: my mother's voice was *very* different when I was small."

Steve could see the quarter-moon through a hole in the low-slung clouds that had closed in on the mountains since nightfall. He blinked his eyes sleepily: was that the shape of the Dragon flying past?

"I wonder what it's like being an angel and living in the stars?" he asked no one in particular, leaning against the wolf-dog until Mara gave a small grunt of pain: her wound was healed, but still tender.

Jewel felt, rather than saw, the clouds beginning to break up overhead.

"Do they look beautiful, Jim, the stars?"

"Yes—"

"I like 'em!" the boy cut in with enthusiasm.

"Why do you like the stars, Steve?" the blind girl asked.

"You can touch 'em."

"Really?" Jewel smiled with mock seriousness.

But the boy was firm, and would allow no doubting:

"That's why I like them!"

Jewel decided to poll the rest of the American contingent.

"Why do *you* like the stars, Jim?"

"Who said I do?"

Jewel smiled. "Me."

She was right, Jim knew that, and he knew the reason why he liked the stars, too. But he needed a few seconds to remember. When he remembered, Jim felt the familiar warm wash of smallness in the face of the infinite.

"I like the stars . . . because . . . I can't touch them. Because I will reach and reach forever and never touch them."

"Don't you ever want to reach them?"

"Naw."

Jewel knew that feeling every time she walked.

"That sounds like the future," she said.

"The future?"

"The past you can touch. Tuan, when he talks about the past, I can feel it, I *know* it."

Jim was lost for a moment.

"Tuan? Oh, yes, your—"

"Friend—he only talks about the past." Jewel stared into the orange flames of the campfire, seeing nothing. "I like it, but I like to have hope, too."

In the flickering light of the campfire, deep within the surrounding trees, the soft eyes of the Dragon watched.

Alta could not stop humming the soft melody: it annoyed Tai Ching, it soothed her.

They sat at her table, cleared now of all signs that the American's notes and maps had littered its surface for a week. Four arrows were laid across the table, arrows especially fashioned by Tai Ching. He had spent the past hour continually realigning them, for no reason, millimeter by millimeter, outlining their qualities, going over the plan he and Alta had begun to develop. Alta watched him, her head close to the table, resting on a fist, humming.

Both of them felt the strong undercurrent of excitement that tore at every ordinary word they uttered. They were negotiating for their futures, and they both knew it.

"I am not a discriminating man: the trap can be anywhere," Tai Ching tossed out with elaborate unconcern.

"The Dragon's lair." Alta's curt insistence cut his argument short.

"I only need it dead!"

"Not 'it'—*him*. Him, him, him!" Alta's fist clenched tighter, but she did not raise her head. "If the Dragon is attracted to Jewel, he is male—and I need him dead *inside* his cave."

Tai Ching bent his head down close to Alta's.

"You do not always make this an easy partnership!"

Alta turned her head away.

"I do not want to see your eyes: let me dream that this will work."

"My eyes!" Tai Ching straightened up, ready to strike her, as he had so many times in Paris. "You were wrong once already! My eyes!" He could not hit her. Not here, not in this situation. Tai Ching could wait. He had waited ten years.

Alta closed her eyes.

"No, I was not wrong. I did not look in your eyes when I thought you would be dead."

Tai Ching anxiously, compulsively reordered the four arrows. Preparation was necessary. This conversation was simply to pass time until Alta would be ready to make the girl lead them to the Dragon.

"You did not see it in my eyes," he said with irritation. "Then why did you think that I would die?"

"I paid for it."

Alta turned to face Tai Ching now, coldly assured. She did not look in his eyes, but at the expression of betrayal that smeared his mouth.

"You need me now," she said with matter-of-fact firmness. "And when we kill the Dragon, you will need me even more."

It was said that even during the bad old days of the worst Stalinist repressions the Gypsies could bring anything one wanted into Karistan—for the right price. Then, because Karistan was surrounded by mountains, even without the Gypsies the borders had always been "soft"—it is a worldwide fact that mountain people from every race, culture, nation, or regime respect only one border: the weather that closes the passes with snow in winter, with flash floods and landslides the rest of the year. Beautiful color televisions from Japan had been found in the homes of successful black market money changers for a decade before the People's Republic of Karistan had officially opened trade restrictions. Crime, which seemed to appear hand in glove with the introduction of Western-style economic reforms, had established itself decades before that.

It had not been difficult, then, for Karita to arrange three vehicles and a score of weapons to be at Doc's disposal. It was not cheap, but it had not been a problem. Of course the volume and the hurry would attract eventual attention, but Karita expected to be out of the country by the next afternoon. Doc would drive across the border by nightfall to meet her. The bunch of "soldiers" he had recruited in Vavel that afternoon were expendable: Frank Brown's MERCO project was worth more in a day than the whole lot in a lifetime.

The vehicles were large, Land-Rover types, with powerful engines whose roars cut the air as the small caravan moved through the night, speeding over the rolling hills from Vavel to Grodo, coming to a stop just outside the village.

Doc drove the lead Rover. He wanted one vehicle to himself.

He killed his headlights and waited for the drivers of the two following Rovers to do the same. Then he stepped out of the Rover and walked back to the last vehicle in the line.

"Half of you, out here!" he said forcefully. They were all carrying loaded weapons now; he wanted no one getting ambitious on him.

Several Vavelkos jumped out of the vehicle, stumbling about in the dark, and made even more dangerous by their annoyance at doing so. Doc pulled over one of the Vavelkos that had been identified as an English speaker. "Translate," he ordered.

He faced the group.

"You can drink as much as you need to stay warm, but I want you sober by sunrise." He added with emphasis: "The farmers get up at sunrise!"

Doc waited for the translation to be made. He had been through this routine before. Hell, when was the last time—in Iraq? Yeah, Iraq. That had been a good consulting job. Running in with the Iraqis to check out the Iranian oil fields they'd captured. A patriotic stint, too: it was good to be an advisor in the pay of Uncle Sam—and MERCO. Couldn't forget Frank "Sugar Daddy" Brown, man who could line up a contract and pull out the minerals, oil—hell, even Afghani diamonds!—under fire and ahead of schedule. Time to get back to order-giving. He waved his arm at the single road:

"No Americans, no cars, leave here tomorrow until I say they do. Very simple to understand, nothing else."

Not every job was so much fun, though: the guy would probably just take the buy-off tomorrow and all this would be unnecessary.

Doc turned to the driver of the last Rover:

"Take the rest to the other side of town and plug up the road there." He shot a quick glance at the Vavelkos still in the Rover. "Same rules as here!" he ordered.

Day after tomorrow, I'll have the papers and put them

straight. Doc liked paperwork. He liked science. It was important to do a thorough job—every time—important to get the right results—every time. That's where he and Frank Brown saw eye-to-eye.

Doc stepped out to a point where everyone could see him. It was time for the important address of the operation:

"Anybody screws up, I will kill them."

He tossed two bottles of Karistan brandy into the dirt near the feet of his first post roadblock guards, then climbed into his Rover and led the reduced caravan into the darkness.

CHAPTER 21
Choice

Tcht-tcht-tcht.

"If I had wings/Like Nora's dove—"

Tcht-tcht-tcht.

"I'd fly to heaven/For the girl I love—"

"Mr. Brown?"

"Yes, Mrs. Fiddler?"

"I can keep one of the girls late to type these up."

Tcht-tcht-tcht.

"No hurry. Take a look at this."

The Chief Secretary for the MERCO Executive Pool made her way across the empty conference room to the window where CEO and President Frank Brown stood. He was looking out through the venetian blinds into a late afternoon haze of sunlight.

Tcht-tcht-tcht.

"Yes, Mr. Brown?"

A nod of the head. The Chief Secretary looked down towards the indicated site: the lawn surrounding the corporate headquarters building was being sprinkled by an automatic watering system.

Tcht-tcht-tcht.

"I'm watching them water the concrete."

More precisely: the sidewalk was receiving the main benefits of the sprinkler system.

"I'll have them turn off the water, Mr. Brown, wasting—"

"No problem."

Tcht-tcht-tcht.

"It's amazing the hopes of people in this country."

The Chief Secretary nodded in vague agreement, then left. Frank Brown resumed singing softly to himself. Southern Blues. The best.

"Fare thee well/Oh, Liza!

"Fare—thee—well."

The morning was bright and clear, with only a slight cover of dew wetting the grass about the village. As always, life had started early in Grodo. It always starts early in a farm village, yawned the Superintendent, stepping gingerly over a mud slick and across the main road towards the Village Committee Meeting Hall. He stopped three-quarters of the way across at the sight of a Rover parked next to the building—with an (obviously) American man sleeping behind the driver's wheel. Sturi shrugged: Mr. Marlowe must have been more effective with his call to America than he realized. Excitement began to creep into the Superintendent's thoughts, but he pushed any speculations down and entered the Village Committee Meeting Hall. There were papers to be filed for the weekly report to Vavel. Let the sleeping American wake up to his own sore bones and come to the administration office when he was ready.

Doc opened his eyes as soon as the stubby little local official had disappeared into the grey slab Commie commissar building. He had been seen: that was good—he was the distraction. Doc sat up in his seat and surveyed the village:

Two of his Vavelkos stood near the tavern eating sausages they had just bought.

At the far end of town, Hammer Hands—Doc liked the man, even if he had been easy prey for a sucker punch—was stopping a farm wagon and casually checking the exiting peasant's load.

Four other Vavelkos were scattered about the main street.

This checked out, Doc climbed from the Rover and began changing his outer garments: tie, sports coat, and briefcase were added to complete the portrait of a visiting American technical consultant. Doc followed the Superintendent's footsteps into the Village Committee Meeting Hall. He liked countries like this: the system was just made to be taken advantage of.

"We don't get to ride a truck this time?"

Steve plopped down the gym bag containing his key belongings: three pocket video games.

"Too much important stuff to take back. Superintendent's driving us," Jim answered, dropping his own set of suitcases in front of the State Country House.

"I liked the wagon."

"Power to you, kid." Jim set one bag apart from the rest of the pile he had been building up for the past ten minutes.

"What's that, Dad?" Steve asked from his general's seat atop the footlocker holding geological equipment.

His father answered with a sheepish grin:

"Something we're going to leave with Jewel—give us a reason to come back."

That was a sore point, one no one had wanted to discuss for the past two days. Leaving Jewel. Jim and Steve had no rights, Jim knew that. And Jewel had made no protests to indicate she was dissatisfied with her current situation. But it was a waste—of talent and character and . . . Jim hated sounding melodramatic, but it was true—it was a waste of a *life* for the blind girl to be living as she was, where she was. Besides, Steve liked her. And in a few years—only two or three, really—maybe Jim could . . . could, too.

The wolf-dog heard the approaching Rover first.

Mara was standing next to Steve by the time the Rover appeared on the road. Both were standing apart from Jim when the vehicle stopped in front of the State Country

House and disgorged its two occupants. One of them was a very confused Superintendent.

"Mr. Marlowe!" Sturi said with a rush as he stumbled out of the Rover, "this man says he is from your company. He is Doctor Lawrence Westmore."

Jim stiffened at both bits of information.

"Doc," he identified tersely.

Doc extended his hand in greeting—

"I . . . did not know that we'd met."

—it was a gesture that Jim did not acknowledge.

"We haven't. But I've had to work for companies that bid against your reports. Why are you here?"

"We work for the same company now.

Jim turned to Steve.

"Take that one bag over to Jewel. Take Mara with you. I'll be over there a few minutes behind you." He gave his attention back to Doc. "This won't take long, will it?" he asked aggressively.

Doc shook his head. He felt good. He felt The Edge.

"It won't take long."

The boy and the wolf-dog stood watching the adults.

"Go on now, Steve!" Jim urged.

Steve gave a halfhearted tug at the bag.

"It's too big!"

"Then go without it—I'll bring it in a minute. Go on!"

Steve understood that no excuses would work to keep him from going.

"OK, OK, OK, OK," the boy jabbered. Followed by Mara, he headed for the forest path that led to Alta's house—and where Jewel waited disconsolately to see them off.

Jim watched them disappear from sight—he trusted his son, but not the boy's curiosity—then turned back to face Doc.

"Inside."

Without waiting for a response, Jim walked into the cabin. The Superintendent followed on his heels. Doc appraised the door for a moment, decided it was safe to enter, then stepped in lightly.

Upon entering the one-room cabin, his eyes took immediate note of the stack of maps and papers piled on the table near the kitchen area. Doc looked at Jim, then at the Superintendent. A witness. The only witness so far—not counting the kid. Doc wanted to make his words sound official, official words for the official scab wasting space in the room. He nodded "officially" to the Superintendent, then began his spiel to Marlowe:

"We can make this very short if you want: Frank Brown has authorized me to pay you the balance of your fee in return for the reports—and to advise you that the reports are the legal property of the company."

Jim felt his muscles untense. He had not known what to expect, had not expected anyone from MERCO to show up in Grodo. They had hired in Doc. Jim felt a contempt for Frank Brown he had not dared feel before. Talk about your standards!

"You can always pay me—" Jim tried to smile, knowing this was the catchphrase of the Docs: he was too nervous to manage more than a spastic tic at the corners of his mouth. "But the company gets its copy of the reports along with everyone else: the government of Karistan and the U.S. government."

Doc felt The Edge sharpen.

"You don't even have to sign the reports: I'll prepare the final version."

"No, that's OK—I'll sign them."

"And how will they be presented?"

"In full detail."

Doc let out a pleasant sigh. Now to threat—

Doc remembered the presence of the Superintendent. He smiled at the nuisance, still addressing his words to Jim Marlowe.

"They will be—misinterpreted . . . I am also authorized to double your fee."

Jim said nothing. After a moment, Doc turned away from both men and stepped outside the cabin. He stood out in the bright sunlight and made a slow 360-degree circle, spinning on his heel, finally turning to face the darkened

interior where the dim outlines of Marlowe and the Superintendent indicated that they were watching him intently.
Doc began to speak sincerely—to the trees:

"There will come a day, Jim Marlowe, when you will
go before a board or a government agency—and it will be
a day like any other day, a hearing like any other
hearing—and you will go in with all of your facts and figures and very sincere convictions. And you will tell these
facts and figures and very sincere convictions to those
people . . . and you will see in their faces that they do not
need to listen to you. They had made their decisions long
before: to get this particular vote, that particular new car,
a promotion. Whatever you say makes no difference to
them . . . at all. Is there a future generation? Don't ask the
people—the nice, gentle people—don't ask them to help
you fight for the future. They won't."

Doc moved closer to the cabin, speaking to the dim outline of Marlowe that hovered just inside the doorway.

"Do you want to face that day?"

Jim stepped out of the cabin. He had understood every
word Doc said.

"I don't have a choice."

"You always have a choice."

Jim looked back into the cabin, at the pile of maps and
documents stacked across the table. A look of chagrined
resignation crossed his face.

"No, I don't."

At this, Doc turned businesslike. It was time to leave, he
knew. No intelligent transactions would be negotiated with
Jim Marlowe. Frank Brown had chosen the wrong puppy.
Bad for Frank Brown. Bad for Jim Marlowe.

A certain relaxation came over Doc then, The Edge
massaging his muscles in relief that a decision point had
been reached and passed. It *was* time to go, but before
doing so, Doc nodded his head in the direction of the little
Superintendent and asked Marlowe:

"He knows?"

"Enough," Jim replied. Then, misreading Doc's inten-
tions, he added:

"In an hour the whole village will know." He smiled with sarcastic triumph. "A lot of people for Frank Brown to buy off."

"Oh, Frank Brown doesn't buy off people in lots." Jim was surprised to see Doc smile in response. "He prefers a more cost-effective approach."

With that parting comment, Doc climbed into the Rover and sped away.

"I think maybe I should have come in my own car, Mr. Jim," observed the Superintendent from the cabin doorstep.

Jim's observation was equally pragmatic.

"I think maybe we should get to Vavel as soon as possible."

CHAPTER 22
Auld Lang Syne

It was easy, Doc thought. Just do the most audacious act without hesitation and nothing can stop you. That's what Frank Brown would do. Doc leaned against the tree and looked out through the undergrowth at Marlowe's cabin. That's what Frank Brown would do.

Marlowe and the little government ass had still been standing in front of the cabin when Doc had returned. It had only taken three, maybe four minutes to drive the Rover back along the dirt road, over a small rise and out of sight, park it, then cut through the forest at an angle to arrive back at the cabin. Would have been faster, Doc knew, if he had not had to take the minimal precaution of keeping relatively quiet. That hadn't been difficult: except for the thin border of undergrowth near the tree line, the majority of the forest floor around the cabin was carpeted in pine needles and mosses that drank up footstep sounds thirstily. Doc had returned in time to see Marlowe cast an uncomfortable glance up at the dirt road, then disappear into the cabin, followed by the Superintendent a moment later. For Doc now, it was all a matter of watch, wait—and then act. Just like Frank Brown would do.

Just like Frank Brown would do.

Doc found himself thinking more and more of Frank Brown, wondering if he thought of the man as a role model or a nemesis. He shook his head and resisted the urge to recheck the action on his rifle: the metallic noise of the bolt sliding into place would be out of sorts with the other forest sounds. Doc had felt hurt when this Marlowe guy was chosen for the Karistan Project. Why had it bothered him so? He was freelance. "I've got no claims on Frank Brown," Doc muttered aloud, then caught himself before clicking his tongue. Stupid lack of concentration! It came from pulling in so many crap amateurs on this gig, he berated himself. If this had been any place in Latin America or the States—or even Western Europe—he could have recruited ready mercenaries with pro-time experience. Don't even talk about the Big Mid-E and Southeast Asia: seemed like every other fourteen-year-old knew the trade in those places!

These Vavelkos weren't bad muscle, though, just not co-ordinated. Maybe next year, when MERCO had the Project in full swing, Doc could recommend a good organizer who would whip these guys into shape and make sure there'd be no labor problems in Karistan. That was Frank Brown's way: pay off the key figures and do anything else necessary to keep the rest in line. But that was the future, not Doc's area of interest. Here it was straightforward: suppress the reports any way necessary, eliminate witnesses. So far, only two. Easy. Then disappear. Cost-effective. Practical. That's what Frank Brown would do.

"I'll go get my son while you get your car."

Doc instinctively raised the barrel of his rifle: Marlowe and the Superintendent were emerging from the cabin. Not yet, he reminded himself.

"I do not want to go to the witch's house," the Superintendent said, emphasizing his words with a spitting gesture.

Marlowe secured a padlock on the front door of the cabin.

"OK, I can understand that. We'll meet you back here."

The Superintendent was already walking up the dirt road away from the cabin.

"I will be in not many minutes, Mr. Jim."

Doc saw Marlowe step away from the cabin and follow

the Superintendent along the road for a few moments, then cut across a field and disappear into a stand of trees. Further on, higher up the mountain, Doc could see a house in that direction. The "witch's house," he assumed, adding a muffled chuckle to his reaction.

On the dirt road, the Superintendent disappeared over the small rise.

Doc began counting silently to himself. Timing. He did not want Marlowe or the Superintendent to be too close—or to get too far away. In a few moments the Superintendent would discover the Rover parked along the dirt road, unoccupied. That would hold his attention long enough. Marlowe could see me if he turns to look back at his cabin, Doc thought, but he doesn't have any reason to look back. Not yet.

Time to give Mr. Marlowe a reason to look back.

Doc finally gave in to the urge to click the bolt on the rifle, sliding a bullet into the chamber, then laid the weapon carefully on the ground, the safety off. He pushed his way through the two-meter border of undergrowth and emerged from the forest, across the road from the cabin. There he made a casual survey of the area to confirm that Marlowe and the Superintendent were out of sight. That done, Doc quickly crossed the open space, making his way directly to the cabin.

The padlock on the front door gave Doc approximately a half second's pause for reflection.

"Oughta trust your neighbors, Jim," he joked to the locked door. He did not bother to test the strength of the lock or the door. Instead, Doc stepped over to the nearest window. He pressed his nose against the glass, squinting into the darkened interior.

Yes, there were the reports, still stacked neatly on top of the kitchen table.

To take—or not to take: that was the question. Doc smiled: oh, why?

He slipped on a leather glove, a thick, rig-worker's gauntlet. With his ungloved hand Doc pulled a palm-sized metal object from his jacket pocket. The object was round. The object was an incendiary grenade.

Doc put the grenade into his gloved hand, pulled the pin, then thrust the gloved hand through the window glass. Hand inside the cabin, he tossed the explosive device towards the kitchen table, stepping away from the window almost immediately.

The explosion was, in professional terms, "soft." Doc stood aside from the window a safe two meters and watched the gush of flames burst out. He felt the cabin wall at his back shake from the concussion—and then the rush of explosive excitement was over. Without looking back, Doc walked away from the cabin, across the dirt road, and into the forest.

A "soft" explosion does not mean "silent." Especially in the still mountains. Jim heard the explosion first—there was no obstacle to impede the sound waves' progress. The Superintendent, still standing at the abandoned Rover, heard it second: the sound had bounced over the small rise in the road and hit the Superintendent on its echo three seconds later. Jim looked down the mountain and saw the flames rushing from the cabin windows. The Superintendent saw only the smoke rising above the trees in the direction of the State Country House. Both men began running.

Jim was down the mountain and running across the field to the cabin first. Flames were now belching through the roof. With anxious, fumbling movements he pulled out the key and attempted to unlock the padlock on the front door. The lock was hot and kept burning his fingers as he tried to hold it still. Finally, by enfolding the lock in his bunched-up handkerchief, Jim managed to steady the lock long enough to insert the key and release the bolt.

"No! Don't open it!" the Superintendent shouted from the road, rushing up to the cabin and pulling the American away from the door.

"My papers!" Jim cried. "The damn reports are in there!"

"Maybe they are and maybe they are not!" Sturi shouted back, surprised at his own vehemence in the situation.

"But you will look, Mr. Jim!" and he pointed at the door. True to his warning, flames were already licking at the door's edges.

Jim stepped back away more willingly.

"All right, they're lost," he said. It was a statement without much room for argument.

"There are more old maps in town, Mr. Jim—the important information is in you." Sturi was proud of his observation.

Jim nodded in enthusiastic, grim agreement.

"Then let's call the police."

Oh well, thought the Superintendent, it was nice to be strong for a moment. He gave a wry smile.

"The police—that is me . . ." He added apologetically: "We don't have crime here!" Sturi saw the American Mr. Jim Marlowe's face fall in defeat—until he added with definitive authority: "We can find help in the village, though!"

It worked: Jim's face lit up—his adrenaline rush found a second wind.

"OK, Superintendent."

"Sturi."

"Sturi."

The thud into Sturi's chest came a half instant before the cracking sound. The surprised look on his face seemed to explode with the gunshot. The Superintendent staggered in surprise.

For a moment, a brief moment, Jim and Sturi stared at one another stupidly, the realization of what had happened dawning upon them. Then the Superintendent collapsed.

"The witch was right!" he gasped.

Even as Sturi crumpled to the ground, a second gunshot sound rang out across the mountain air, a bullet clipping Jim's arm lightly as he dived behind the many suitcases and trunks still piled by the side of the dirt road.

Doc cursed the sudden movement by Marlowe that had spoiled his aim. He began reloading the single-action rifle. Slow, evenly spaced shots would eventually find their target. He raised the rifle to his shoulder, narrowing his attention to the telescopic sight. Marlowe could not be seen through the viewfinder, safely hidden behind the luggage stacked near the cabin—but the dying little ass of a Superintendent made matters worse: he was lying in front of those bags, obscuring Doc's line of fire even more.

Jim tried to disappear into the ground. He kept wishing it to happen, pushing himself flatter and flatter against the soft earth and hoping to accomplish the impossible by an act of will. He had never considered his luggage as more than a necessary nuisance before. Now he valued the steel-reinforced suitcases and equipment-filled trunks with a special fervor. These were his wall, his protectors, his bastion, his—

"He . . . will know . . . about your son and the girl . . ."

Jim heard the Superintendent choking out the words, only a meter away—on the other side of the baggage. In the open.

"I told him . . . who . . . had helped."

Jim began to burrow a small passage through the luggage, a way for the Superintendent to crawl back to safety.

"Wait," he whispered. "Wait! Don't move! Let him think you're dead." A bullet shattered the handle of a heavy trunk just above Jim's head. He shoved his face into the ground, a shiver of fear jostling his shoulders. "Wait," Jim called out to reassure the Superintendent. He was almost crying, forcing himself to raise his head.

He shoved at a small opening—he could see the Superintendent's hand—made the opening wider. A bullet kicked dirt in his face. Jim shrank back.

"I'm going to push these suitcases apart," he whispered urgently to the Superintendent. "He seems to need about five seconds between shots. Wait till the next shot—then I'll shove."

The next shot tore a corner off the suitcase holding Jim's reference books, springing the lock open, scattering heavy texts across his lap. Jim shoved.

"NOW! Grab my hand, I'll h—"

The Superintendent was dead.

Jim found himself facing Doc, a hundred meters away,

a huge gap pushed open in his baggage-wall. Doc was reloading his rifle with deliberate calm. He raised the rifle.

Jim grabbed at a reference book, pulling it up against
his face. He felt the impact before he heard the sound.

The book slammed against his face, knocking him tumbling back, flying from his fingers, the bullet lodged somewhere between pages 800 and 900. Jim didn't wait an
instant to feel if his nose was broken. He jumped to his
feet and ran like hell in a zigzag pattern towards the cabin,
away from Doc.

Doc knew immediately what Marlowe was doing, and
cursed himself for being lulled into a rhythmic-pattern
sighting and shooting. He loaded the next round in half-
time, raised the rifle, fired—knowing as he did so that it
was too late: Marlowe had safely dived behind the corner
of the burning cabin.

Jim tried to lean against the cabin wall, gasping deep,
painful gulps of air. But the wood was too hot to touch,
spots of blackened wall smoked in angry testimony to the
raging fire within the cabin. These walls would crumble
soon, Jim realized, leaving him exposed—if not hurt by
the falling roof. And the walls were weakened, growing
thinner by the second as fire carved away the innards of
the building. How thick—

Doc's next shot ripped through the two angled walls
at the corner of the cabin, missing Jim by a meter, full
proof that there was no protection here.

Doc, too, saw that time was on his side: Marlowe's
cover would soon be perforated by gunfire. One last shot
with the rifle, just to empty the chamber—then a little
rapid fire from the Uzi slung over his shoulder. That
would be fun, peppering the wall. Probably more humane,
too: Marlowe wouldn't know what had hit him.

He saw the horse standing at least a kilometer away, on
top of the bare rocks that crowned the mountain. Let's
give it a try, Doc thought. If I make it, I make it. If I don't,
it won't affect the job either way. He had The Edge. The
reports were gone. Witness One was gone. Witness Two

about to be ... Then the two kids. They probably didn't know anything. He'd find out and do what was necessary.

Jim crouched low to the ground in a sprinter's start position, waiting. He did not have a choice. The shot would come any moment, and when it did—

It came.

Jim felt himself rushing forward with that falling/flying force that characterized the sprint, his legs pumping, ground whirling past in a blur, holding on to one single mouthful of breath.

Calmly angry at missing the horse, Doc threw aside the empty rifle and unslung the Uzi. Marlowe was making a run for the trees. Doc snapped up the safety on the automatic pistol and opened fire.

Jim saw the trees ahead splinter apart, heard the gunfire crackling its staccato message. He spun on his heel and cut a ninety-degree turn—he would stay in the open a second longer, but he would not be running headfirst into death. The splintering trees drew a path of skidding bullets across the open field to close in on Marlowe's heels.

Then, abruptly, Jim felt the bullets singing about him— and felt their inaccuracy. He had passed out of the Uzi's effective aiming range. There was still danger from a stray shot, but as he passed into the first line of trees and undergrowth Jim realized he had bought some time.

Hunting time, Doc thought, replacing the ammunition clip in the Uzi, and abandoning his cover to begin the open pursuit. As he approached the burning cabin he lifted the dead weight of the Superintendent from the ground, used the body as a shield from the unbearable heat, and hurled it against a blazing wall. The roof would collapse soon, taking evidence of this victim with it.

Doc looked over at the trees: Marlowe was making for the "witch's" house. They could bury Jim Marlowe across the border.

Jim did not like running in a forest, but he could not make himself stop. He had intended to head for the path to Alta's house, to warn Steve and Jewel, but the need to make the right-angle turn had disoriented him. He slammed his shoulder hard against a pine tree, then stopped face-to-face with another tree, uncertain on which side to bypass it. He needed to find the dirt road in order to regain his bearings.

With minimal orientation and blind luck, Jim found the dirt road cutting through the forest in front of him. Suddenly fearful of losing the cover of trees, he stopped to catch his breath, then sprinted across the empty space. He knew where he was now.

Jim began to travel at a slower, jogging pace through the forest, parallel to the road. He had traveled a quarter-kilometer that way when he saw the men.

Jim wanted to cry with relief when he first saw them, grouped around a Rover by the side of the road. But his throat was too racked with the salty taste of exertion. He could only run silently towards them.

Finally he was close enough to rasp out some words:

"Who speaks English here?!" he gasped, causing the men to look away from the bottle of brandy that had held their primary attention. "I need help, the Superinten—"

The men were holding guns.

"Oh . . . shit."

And with that pithy comment, Jim charged past the startled Vavelkos and back into the safe cover of the forest. The men hastily thew away the brandy bottle and—less-than-expecting the sudden arrival of the American—began their pursuit hesitantly. Doc caught up with them before the entire group had left their Rover.

"Get back to the Rover. I'll drive. I know where he's going."

Sounds are strange in the mountains. Some sounds can be heard for miles across a valley, jumping from mountaintop to mountaintop. Other sounds bounce around, plow into cliffs, become lost in the deep blanket of trees that cover the mountainsides. At Alta's house, Steve and Jewel stood outside, making the uncomfortable sounds of parting. They did not hear the sounds of explosion, nor the crackling sounds of gunfire. But as Jim burst from the trees, both the boy and the blind girl had their ears attuned to the sounds of approaching cars coming down the road.

"Get in the house! Get in the house!" Jim shouted wildly as he rushed across the road—and its exposed space—grabbing up Steve in one arm and yanking at Jewel's elbow with the other. His hands full, he kicked open the door violently and thrust them in ahead of him.

Halfway through the door to the kitchen, Tai Ching shoved himself back from the living room as the American flung the boy and girl into the room. Alta, seated at the table in front of Tai Ching's arrows, jerked up from her seat, startled at their entrance. Jim pulled Steve and Jewel into the middle of the room, turned back to the door, and—as Mara loped into the house behind them—closed the door with his shoulder. The next few moments were a confusion of words and noise.

"Jim, what is—!"

"Dad?!"

"No time!" Panting. "No time! . . . Killed the Superintendent!" Jim twisted his head abruptly to face Alta directly, shouting: "They killed the Superintendent!"

Alta felt her stomach knot.

"Who?!"

"Working for Brown—my employer!" Jim stopped trying to talk: he could not breathe. He felt dizzy with the effort. Several long, heaving breaths later, he continued, much slower, speaking to the floor:

"They are going to try to kill everyone who knows about my reports: all of us . . . we have some time." He addressed his next words to Alta. He had been working out the rough outlines of a plan while running through the forest.

"We have some time. You go into Grodo. Get help. Stay there. I'll take Steve and Jewel and hide . . . in the Table Rocks—they won't find us there."

"But we—" Jewel began to protest.

Alta cut in strongly:

"Go with him. Hide out in the caves—I will take care of myself." She turned her attention to Jim.

"Go out the back way, it cannot be seen from the road."
In the kitchen, Tai Ching stepped behind the door.

"You have to come with us now," Jim said. "Make your way down to the village through the forest."

Alta nodded agreement, then led them through the kitchen and out the back door. The forest here ran almost up to the back of the house. They parted company at the tree line, Jim leading Steve, Jewel, and Mara up the steep slope, Alta hesitating a moment—then returning to the house as the others disappeared from sight. She closed the back door and turned to face Tai Ching. He held his crossbow loosely. It was loaded now.

"We will have to protect our investment, I think," he smiled grimly, taking a long-bladed Indonesian kris from its decorative position on the wall.

Jim found that Jewel was guiding them as much as he—and he had learned from the past weeks' experience not to resist her stubborn knowledge of the area. They reached the first small ridge above Alta's house without noticeable resort to an identifiable path. Jim looked back to see how close behind Doc would be.

He saw the Rover pull up in front of Alta's house. Doc and one other man jumped out of the vehicle and rushed towards the door. Both carried automatic weapons. Jim did not waste time on a second look.

Alta stood alone at her table when the two men burst through the door. The arrows were cleared from the table. She looked up expectantly at their entrance, noting that one was a typical Vavel street criminal and the other was dressed like an American. Both carried automatic pistols, the Vavelko in his hands, the American slung across his back. Alta also looked into their eyes.

Doc saw the look of horror cross the woman's face: she knew about them, he realized.

"I think you may know," he said softly, then instructed her like a kindly doctor: "Just close your eyes."

He nodded to the Vavelko, and the man raised his weapon, aiming it at Alta—then he screamed a short burst of agony as the arrow pinned him to the wall!

Doc spun around on the action, reaching for his gun—

"Don't move anymore," Tai Ching commanded from the kitchen doorway.

Doc froze in mid-motion, his face partially turned away from the door.

Tai Ching stepped out from the kitchen, the emptied crossbow in one hand, the long blade of the Indonesian kris gleaming in the other.

"I can cut off your hand before you reach your gun," he continued—then stopped, exclaiming with sudden familiarity:

"Doc! It's you?!"

Doc heard the French-tinged words and relaxed his shoulders, remembering Thailand and the most amoral Chinese he had ever met. He turned to face the smiling Tai Ching.

Tai Ching, for his part, found himself looking from Doc to Alta—and feeling an idea create itself. He continued to point the kris at Doc as three more Vavelkos rushed in through the front door.

"Doc—I think we can save you time."

CHAPTER 23

Neutral Ally

They had to cross a small stream and step out onto a dangerously exposed clearing before Jim could see the house again. There were three Rovers in front of the house now—Doc sitting alone in one, the other two filled with the type of men Jim had run away from minutes before. At a signal from Doc that Jim could only see and not hear, the Rovers started up and pulled away from the house. Now that the vehicles were moving, Jim saw that Doc was not alone in his Rover: he vaguely made out that there were two passengers. Neither sat near enough an open window for Jim to get a better view.

But both figures appeared to be directing Doc: as his Rover hit the dirt road, it turned away from the village and towards the direction of the mountaintop without hesitation.

"Damn!" Jim informed Jewel and Steve, stepping back into the cover of the trees. "I think they're trying to cut us off!" He took Jewel's hand and addressed her directly. "Will the road come between us and the Table Rocks on this side of the mountain? We never crossed up this way before."

Jewel had not been considering specifics as they fled towards the Table Rocks. Now she turned her memory to the feel of the ground as she remembered last walking this route. The soft spring of the pine needles. The loose dust covering once-hard-packed earth. Then the pine needles again.

"Yes," she answered, "the road will cross above us. It does not go all of the way to the Table Rocks, but it lies between us and that point."

She knew she was not giving Jim the answer he wanted to hear.

"We could go back down," she suggested.

But Jim pushed aside a branch and looked intently at the approaching Rovers, studying the occupants of the two vehicles behind Doc. He recalled the faces of the men he had fled: they had been excited faces, dangerous, armed men—but half-drunk and out of their element.

"They won't know their way around a playground," he said to himself with unexpected satisfaction. He added up the pluses and minuses of the fugitives' situation.

"No, there's no place to hide if we go back down: I'm sure he has people looking for us there—" Yeah, he was certain of *that,* Jim thought, recalling his experiences with the Rover and the firebombed cabin. "Besides, your mother should be down in Grodo by now. Someone will get help." He hoped. "If we can get up into the rocks . . ."

Jim stopped, realizing the fantasy behind his words: a blind girl, a small boy—only Mara was fast enough.

"You could make it alone," Jewel said quickly, reading his thoughts.

"Yeah. And I could eat lunch in Paris, too!" Jim snorted. "You ever heard such dumb talk, Steve?"

At this cue the little jabberbox started up.

"Listen, Dad, I have a plan: we could go over the hill, and then over the hill and then over the hill, and then you could beat up those guys, and then over the hill, and—"

Jim put his hand over the boy's mouth.

"Moment, son! We have to get going!"

"Where?" Steve mumbled through Jim's fingers.

Jim gave a last look back at the house, then turned his attention towards the Table Rocks.

"Over the hill," he sighed in resignation.

* * *

"They are going to the Table Rocks," Tai Ching said again, the French inflections requiring a repetition for comprehension.

"Yeah, yeah, and yes," Doc nodded, "and I see them, too. Question is: which way now?"

Tai Ching twisted in his seat to face the back of the Rover.

"*Chère* Alta? This is your expertise."

This was her—very literal—crossroads: the dirt road divided up ahead. Both directions would lead high up the Low Mountains, eventually trailing out near the Table Rocks. But one, the one that *looked* correct from this perspective, would wind back on itself and approach the mountaintop from the other side. The second fork would most assuredly cut across the Americans' path—and Jewel's.

"Take this direction," she said, pointing to the second fork.

Jim had decided to adapt Jewel's advice to their needs: they would go up the mountain by backtracking down. Not far, but back down the steep hill they had just climbed, to the stream. They would follow that stream up the mountain, Jim planned, using the noise of the running water and the steep banks alongside the stream to cover their movements. They needed to abandon Jewel's regular route to the top anyway: the blind girl was leading them faultlessly, but she could not see the distant pursuers and know when her chosen paths were being rendered useless for their purpose of escape. Specifics aside, Jim knew forest travel—and the past weeks' work had given him a fairly decent orientation to the Low Mountains. He felt confident that he could lead them to the Table Rocks faster than Doc and his men would be able to get there. Except for the road. They had to cross the road. And Doc's Rovers would control that before the fugitives could make it that far.

The White Horse was standing at the bottom of the steep hill, drinking from the stream. Steve saw him first.

"Tuan!" he cried, tumbling down the hill and into the

stream without concern. The wolf-dog loped easily along beside the boy, stopping to drink nose-to-nose with the horse. Steve bent down and spoke urgently in the White Horse's ear.

"Tuan! We need your help! There's a lotta bad guys."

Jim slid down the hill less enthusiastically than his son had, helping Jewel with the stiff incline. He looked at the strange-eyed horse incredulously.

"Where did that horse come from?!"

Jewel could hear the varied snorts and movements of the White Horse.

"It is my friend Tuan, that I told you about."

"There's no one here, only a horse," Jim corrected the blind girl, coming up to the magnificent animal and stroking its neck in admiration. It was a short-lived moment of appreciation: the roaring engines of the Rovers crossed the dirt road nearby.

"Then it's Tuan's horse," Jewel stated, disappointed by Jim's failure to perceive the truth.

But Jim had no time for perceptions—of the White Horse or Jewel's emotions—he was beginning to see a way out of the situation.

"I don't care if it's the devil's horse!" he said with sudden dismissal. "Can you ride?"

"I have ridden that horse."

"Good." Jim led Jewel over to the White Horse. "Then you two ride up to the Table Rocks." He helped her onto the animal. "Hide in a cave." He lifted Steve easily onto the horse in front of Jewel. "I'll come as fast as I can."

He slapped the White Horse on the rear to make it run. Jim turned to the wolf-dog and shouted with desperate encouragement: "Go with 'em, Mara!"

He watched them run away, the White Horse following the course of the stream. With luck, Jim thought, they will cross the road farther on than Doc would expect—and sooner. But Jim knew he had to make sure of that.

"He's down there," Doc noted, looking through the binoculars: Jim Marlowe was running like a panic-stricken scarecrow across a clearing not two hundred meters below the road. But Marlowe was alone. What about—?

He turned to his men and shouted frantically:

"Every forty meters—spread out—*SPREAD OUT!* We want the man first, but look out for the kids!"

He pulled his attention rapidly back to the clearing while his order was translated. Even without the binoculars Doc could see Marlowe running back and forth across the clearing—and Marlowe could see him. Standing in one place. Being suckered into not closing off the road. Doc raised the binoculars back up to his eyes and scanned the mountainside above the road. He sighed in minor defeat.

"The boy and your daughter have got a horse."

Tai Ching was at Doc's side anxiously.

"Let me see!"

Doc gave him the binoculars: it was a hunting game now anyway, pulling in the net on Marlowe, then plodding after the other two.

Tai Ching turned the binoculars towards the direction Doc had been looking. He saw nothing at first—then the white flash between some trees. He had difficulty holding the binoculars steady, the forest seemed to dance through the lenses. A second flash of white. Tai Ching gave up trying to find the fugitives among the trees and turned the binoculars towards the clear space between the tree line and the Table Rocks. His foresight was rewarded moments later by the sight of the White Horse and its passengers emerging from the forest at a gallop. There appeared to be a wolf running at the horse's heels. Tai Ching had never seen anything so beautiful as the horse's eyes.

"You were right," he said to Alta, handing her the binoculars.

Doc sent three of the Vavelkos fanning out down the mountainside in the direction of Marlowe, then returned to Tai Ching and Alta. He pointed over the woman's shoulder towards the Table Rocks: the White Horse and its passengers were visible to the naked eye—but barely.

"We'll pick them up later," he nodded to Alta.

Through the binoculars Alta saw the White Horse carry Jewel and Steve into the Table Rocks.

Doc was impatient to get after Marlowe. "You give your word for the girl?" he demanded. He wanted assurance from Tai Ching's moody partner.

"We won't have to," Alta answered with distant satisfaction.

The White Horse made its way with precision through the twists and turns of the Table Rocks, followed closely by Mara. Steve recognized the way. Jewel, deprived of her usual sensory references, could only guess at the general directions. In fact, she had never been down this particular series of passages before. Steve had: it was the way to the Dragon's lair.

The White Horse stopped at the entrance to the long shaft that would lead from the Table Rocks passages deep into the cavernous lair.

"You are safe here," Jewel heard the voice whisper through the echoing chambers.

"Tuan! You came!"

"Yes."

Jewel hugged Steve, who looked at her strangely. The blind girl began to speak in an excited tumble of words:

"You have to go help Jim—Steve's father! He is out there, on the mountain, and—"

"No."

"—he needs . . ." Jewel only then realized what she had heard.

"No, it . . ." She stumbled over the abrupt refusal. ". . . it's Steve's father." Her voice grew louder, more insistent. "People are trying to kill him. You have to help stop them!"

"I will not take the side of one man against another."

Refused again, Jewel read the wrong reasons of altruism in Tuan's words. She began to plead.

"Tuan, help him!"

"No."

And the White Horse began carrying Jewel and Steve

deeper into the cavern, past the hanging stalactites. Jewel rode in numb silence, hugging Steve for comfort.

The boy sat atop the White Horse's back in angry silence.

Mara trailed reluctantly behind, watching morosely as the White Horse carried the two humans deeper into its home. The wolf-dog could see the blind girl's despairing face and her boy's angry visage. She was not surprised when Jewel cried out:

"Tuan!"

The White Horse ignored the blind girl's cry.

He could not ignore the boy wrestling loose from Jewel's arms and sliding off his back.

"I'm not going with you!" Steve shouted angrily, stalking back towards the entrance.

"Boy!" the voice admonished.

Steve whirled around to face the White Horse, Mara beside him in his resolve.

"I'm going back to my Dad!"

The eyes of the White Horse colored, grew cloudy again. He considered his next words.

"I could stop you," Steve heard at last.

But, at this, Jewel slid off the White Horse's back.

"Can you stop me, too?" she taunted, stumbling in the direction she had heard Steve's voice come from. In a few long seconds she felt the boy's hand grab hold of hers— the wolf-dog brushed against her other side, and the three began walking away from the White Horse, heading back to the mouth of the cavern.

"Do not go." It was a simple statement.

Jewel considered hesitating; the boy did not. They continued walking.

Tuan's words were repeated, this time with a slight edge of emotion.

"Do not go."

Mara led the way: her senses were better than the boy's eyes in the dim-lit shaft. Jewel and Steve had found a co-ordinated walking rhythm. The threesome continued on their way out. Each heard the whispered voice plead:

"You will hurt him!"

Jewel hesitated—she did not turn around to face Tuan, but she stopped walking.

"He needs help," the girl said.

Tuan picked up on her concern, but not to take advantage of it.

"You cannot help him: if you go out, you will only be in his way."

At this, Steve turned around, angry and worried, to face the White Horse.

"He's my Dad!" he shouted. His voice bounced in ringing echoes through the cavern, the words repeated several times.

The White Horse shuffled his feet, his hooves scraping against the stone floor. His eyes met the wolf-dog's, read there a loyalty and understanding of man he had never had the luxury to learn. His mate had tried—her efforts had killed her. He turned his eyes back to the boy.

"He is yours, isn't he." It was not a question.

"Uh-huh," Steve nodded with assurance.

The eyes of the White Horse colored, looked to the girl: she was still facing away.

"He is mine, too," Jewel said.

The White Horse whinnied, stamped its feet, turned its eyes once again towards the animal at the boy's side. Suddenly the wolf-dog turned and ran out of the cavern.

"Mara!?" Steve cried in surprise.

"She will help him to come here," Jewel heard Tuan's voice reassure the boy. "When he is here I will help him . . ." Jewel felt the next words directed at her. "You cannot help him out there."

Jewel tasted once again the bitter reality of helplessness. She touched Steve's shoulder: the boy was sobbing silently, shaking with emotion.

"He is right" were the only lame words of consolation she could offer.

CHAPTER 24

The Closing Net

The wolf-dog padded her way up the shaft and out into the relative openness of the passageways. Mara relied totally on instinct at this point, her eyes unadjusted to the brighter light, her sense of smell useless in the uniform stone dampness of the Table Rocks. She was not slowed down by those obstacles. Her wolf blood knew the way.

Mara emerged from the half-light of the Table Rocks into the full brightness of the mountain. Her ears very easily picked up the sounds of pursuit that hounded her human. The smell of cordite from the cabin explosion hung over the entire mountain like a faint obscenity. She turned her huge head to and fro, scanning the forest below for signs of the hunters' prey.

Doc would have wished for more experienced men, but he had no complaints about their numbers. He had recruited enough Vavelkos to spread out a search line and close off that part of the dirt road immediately above where he knew Marlowe was hiding. He did not worry about Tai Ching and the woman: they had left in pursuit of the boy and the woman's daughter. Doc's interest was on the Big Chase. He felt The Edge sharpen every one of his senses.

It did not do so well with his men.

Jim crouched into a tight ball beneath a pile of brush that leaned against a large rock, cramming his body into a

third of its size. Only footsteps away he could see the bob-
bing head of a dark-haired pursuer as the Vavelko passed
by the pile of brush, more intent on trying to look every
which direction at once than in really seeing what was
around him. Could he have had the luxury of breathing
more than the quiet shallow breaths necessary at the moment, Jim would have sighed in relief at this confirmation
of his earlier assessment of his pursuers: they were dangerous men, but they knew nothing about the wilderness. Except for Doc. Doc would know as much as Jim did about
wilderness surveys, about observation, about how to walk
in the forest. Against the Vavelkos' noisy crashing through
the undergrowth, Jim had to balance the unknown silence
of Doc. Doc could be anywhere. It would be safest, then,
to remain curled up where he was, Jim knew. Let the
search line try to flush him out, pass him by, and then lose
him in the vastness of the forest.

But Doc would know that Steve and Jewel were somewhere up in the Table Rocks. Jim knew that they had
made it past the dirt road—he had heard some of the men
shouting at them in the distance—but he could not count
on a small boy and a blind girl to evade an organized
search headed by Doc. Jim could. He had to leave his safe,
albeit cramped, hiding spot and make a run for the Table
Rocks.

Jim watched the dark-haired pursuer walk out of his
limited line of vision, then listened with aching concentration until the man's loud footsteps faded away further
down the mountainside. Then Jim rolled out from under
the brush and crawled—downhill. He would use the same
strategy he had planned before coming across the horse: to
find the stream and use the cover of its steep banks to run
up the mountain and cross the dirt road at a point much
further over on the mountain than Doc's search line could
stretch. It felt slightly at odds with his emotions to be
crawling away from the Table Rocks, but when Jim found
himself sliding down the steep bank into the stream, he
rose to his feet confident that his plan was sound.

It was.

To a point.

Jim slogged quickly upstream, alerted to the approach of any Vavelkos by their loud progress through the forest, hiding against the steep banks occasionally, but generally uninhibited in his escape from the search line. Until he came to the dirt road.

Jim had been right in his speculation about the search line: Doc did not have enough men to stretch out as far as the point where the stream crossed the dirt road. He had failed to consider that Doc would set up a secondary, wider-spaced cordon along the road itself. Now Jim saw clearly that it was impossible to cross the exposed space: the third Rover was rapidly passing back and forth along the road, dropping off a man every two hundred meters.

Jim squatted down behind the safety of the stream bank. His options were narrowing.

Mara had stood longer than she intended at the entrance to the Table Rocks, her human more elusive of his pursuers than she had expected. Finally the wolf-dog spotted the general area of the hunters' prey and began her silent trot down the mountain to help him. She began to anticipate the taste of the blood hunt.

Mara's attention had been too concentrated upon the immediate danger—or else Tai Ching and Alta carried a more "animal" scent than most humans: the wolf-dog did not notice them in hiding within the forest. As she disappeared into the forest, Alta and Tai Ching emerged from the tree line at a different point. They had seen the Table Rocks entrance Mara had stepped out from, a confirmation of Alta's earlier observation. They walked into the correct entrance themselves and began their passage towards the Dragon's lair.

Doc knelt before the pile of brush and ran his hand over the scratched earth angrily: how anyone could have missed seeing a six-foot man hiding behind *that* was beyond Doc's comprehension. He looked scornfully at the dark-haired Vavelko who had walked by Marlowe. The idiot was drunk! Doc straightened up and pushed the man back roughly.

"Waste my time!" he spat, raising his gun. The Vavelko shrank back even further than Doc had pushed him—until Doc continued to raise his weapon, pointed it at the air, then fired several shots.

"LISTEN!" Doc emphasized the word with a crack of gunfire. "LISTEN! NO—MORE—ALCOHOL!" His shouts echoed through the forest. "I—WILL—KILL—THE NEXT MAN—WHO DRINKS!"

His warning was too late. A bullheaded Vavelko posted along the road stopped in mid-gulp from his bottle when he heard the bullet-emphasized order—but the large stone in Jim Marlowe's hand crashed down on his skull without heed. Jim did not bother to check if the man was alive or dead. He pulled the road guard into the underbrush and ripped the Uzi from the man's unconscious fingers, then greedily searched the bullhead's pockets for ammunition clips. He found a handful. Jim's eyes glinted at this small victory as he crouched into a sprint position.

"All right, Steve, Jewel," he whispered in encouragement to himself, "now we don't have to be just rabbits!"

He sprinted away from the dirt road and back into the forest.

"This way . . . I said this way . . . this . . . here—"

It was only Alta, of course, who was able to follow the tracks of the White Horse through the unimpressed stone passageways of the Table Rocks.

Tai Ching felt the mild annoyance he always endured when dealing with the magic ones, their self-assured abilities rubbing wrongly against his merely mortal attempts to accomplish the same objectives. He massaged his irritated ego with the reminder that he was using Alta.

They passed at last through the maze, to arrive at a seemingly dead end. The passage here was wider than before, but blocked by a large boulder. Tai Ching let out an intentionally "involuntary" whistle in sarcastic deference to Alta's pathfinding skills, a melody that turned to one of astonishment as she walked behind the boulder and called for him to follow.

The entrance to the Dragon's lair was there, Tai Ching had no doubts. He hefted the crossbow in his hands, but knew he had time.

There was no need for Alta to lead down the first section into the lair: the long, prosaic mine shaft was straight and easy to follow. Dull, in fact, made to seem longer to both by the anticipation each held anxiously within. It was not until the shaft widened into the first chamber, where wooden supports were replaced by crystalline stalactites, that they found the first sign of fortune: a precious gem lay gleaming on the salt-laced stone floor.

Tai Ching grabbed up the jewel with a hoot of conquest, turning to face Alta with a satisfied air.

"Did you ever imagine Fort Knox?" he demanded in rapid French. "Did you? With its rooms piled high with the fortune of a nation ... I will fill this chamber with the gold from my fortune!" He looked down at the gem in his hand almost lovingly. "And you—I will keep you here as the symbol of my first piece of this fortune."

He placed the jewel down on the ground: it glowed a deep and beautiful green.

They were deep within the cavern now—Jewel, Steve, and the White Horse—within that grotto that was the Dragon's Lair itself, where the floor was ankle-deep in precious stones and the walls hung heavy with the jeweled hides of Tuan's long-dead companions. Steve lay heavily on the White Horse's back, his eyes dead with depression. At the animal's feet, Jewel knelt in the gems, idly lifting them up with her hands and letting them sift through her fingers. Her face, too, was cast in a look of depression as she listened to Tuan's words of attempted comfort.

"... the right decision is not always ... *right*. Everything in your heart, in your mind, may tell you that there is another way. But an instinct tells you that there is only one right way. It has to be difficult—or everyone would do right ..."

Gradually, as the White Hose allowed his eyes to leave the girl, they focused upon the dark dragon skin hanging nearby, painted across in the Chinese style: the portrait of a Black Horse with strange eyes . . .

"You must trust that instinct, which is older than memory. You must, even if it hurts—"

"Will he make it to us?" Jewel's words fell with the same dead weight as the stones from her hand.

"I do not know. Are there many against him?"

"I think yes."

Steve grew restless upon the White Horse's back.

"He is your father, boy: believe in that."

Jewel turned her lifeless eyes to face the voice. There was an edge of recrimination to her tone.

"Your words do not help, Tuan, even if you are right."

The line of bullets sparked across the boulder—behind which crouched Jim, his back pressed hard against the stone.

Jim could not understand why he wanted to spit in disgust at his stupidity, yet felt his mouth dry with fear. He was safe for the moment—the Vavelko would not run into the small "box" of boulders after Jim—but he had allowed himself to become trapped in the same box he had dived into for protection, pinned down by the wildly firing city thug now starting to call for Doc—as if Doc hadn't already heard the gunfire and was on his way with reinforcements.

"Over here! Over here!" the shooter cried, his high-pitched words alternating with bursts of gunfire to keep the American pinned down. "I've got him trapped! Over here! I've got him! I've got—"

He stopped shouting at the sound of the deep-throated growl. He even stopped shooting, twisting his head rapidly to face the source of the sound. He saw the teeth first, then the eyes of the wolf—only inches from his head—looking down at him.

The shooter tried to turn quickly and face the beast, but Mara jumped immediately, her jaws open to tear at the man's throat. The Vavelko was lucky: his attempt to turn made him fall before the wolf-dog made full impact, her snapping teeth taking only a part of his ear and knocking him sprawling back. He scrambled to his feet after the initial knockdown—his gun was somewhere on the ground—but he did not stop to retrieve the weapon, nor to attempt a stand against the attacking beast. The Vavelko opted instead to run for all he was worth away from the vision of death he had just evaded.

At the cease of gunfire, Jim jumped out from behind his protective, trapping boulder, ready to shoot. He stopped himself with a sudden cry:

"Mara!"

That was the extent of time allowed for his wonder at the wolf-dog's appearance, for almost at once the sounds of near pursuit burst forth from the surrounding forest.

"Over there! He's trapped! Over—"

Jim did not understand a word of the Karistinian language the Vavelkos were shouting, but he gathered the gist of the message—and he had no intention of being pushed back into a trap again. As two of the pursuers broke through the brush, he sent them jumping back with a burst of rapid fire from his Uzi, using his precious ammunition supply to quick effect. Without checking to see *how* effective—one crouched behind a tree and one in full retreat—Jim turned and ran the opposite direction—

"C'mon, Mara!" he shouted, scrambling over the boulder he had recently used for protection. It was time to make the break across the exposed space of the dirt road. It was time to get up to the Table Rocks.

Bullets splashed futile dust bombs over the road as Jim dashed across. His luck had held so far: Doc had not been able to bring the search line back up the mountain fast enough.

But with Jim's desperate run came an exposure that left little guesswork for Doc. There was no need to make a systematic search through the forest now, he calculated, Marlowe was heading for the Table Rocks in full view.

With a few terse orders, Doc reversed his entire team towards the Table Rocks and in running pursuit.

Holding the Uzi in one hand and pumping his arms and legs like an Olympic sprinter, Jim ran up the forested incline that represented the last remaining stand of trees before the Table Rocks. He had no choice: to his far sides—both sides—those of Doc's men who had been guarding the road and saw him dash across it had started running after him as well. As he approached the Table Rocks the natural angle of the mountain curved in: they would close the net on him if they could keep pace. His chances depended on the slim advantage that he had started up the mountain with a slight lead, and the fact that each of his pursuers wasted their time by stopping to take out-of-range shots in his direction. Jim twisted erratically to discourage their aim, but concentrated primarily on maintaining his lead. The Table Rocks presented his only hope of cover.

Doc did not bother running: he wanted a clean shot at the rabbit. He knew where Marlowe was heading—and there was a wide clearing between the tree line and the covering boulders of the Table Rocks. Doc waited patiently for the prey to run into his sights.

Jim saw the clearing through the trees, Mara running ahead of him to the Table Rocks a few short seconds beyond. He broke through the tree line and sprinted for the first opening he could see between the boulders.

Doc was ready when Marlowe burst into the open. He adjusted his leading aim to the fugitive's pace, ready to squeeze—

"Damn idiots!" Doc shouted, raising his head up from the gunsight with a jerk. His own men had become the chief obstacle to his success, running across his projected line of fire! "Stop running! Stop! We know where he's going! Stop!"

Jim made it to the cover of the Table Rocks in an unusual silence: Doc's angry shouts had momentarily halted the pursuit. But only momentarily. Even as Jim reached the protection of the boulders two Vavelkos who had been closest on his heels decided to ignore Doc's command and crashed through the tree line after the fugitive. With the entrance to a passage safely before him, Jim spun on his heel and fired a raking blast at those first-comers, seeing them go down in sudden surprise at their own deaths. Jim quickly swallowed down the bile of repulsion at what he had just done, then turned and followed Mara into the maze of passageways.

The small clearing between the tree line and the entrance to the Table Rocks stood quiet, marked only by the soft moan of the two dying men Jim had left behind. Further down the mountainside, deep within the trees, an occasional figure quickly darted from the cover of one tree to the next.

In contrast, walking at a steady pace without stopping to check for cover, Doc strode through the tree line and up to the bodies of the two fallen pursuers. He turned his attention from the past—they were dead, certainly no part of the future—to look up at the passage that Marlowe had retreated into. After a moment of evaluation he turned back to the rest of his men, still hiding behind the trees.

"He's not here anymore," Doc said with dismissal.

As the Vavelkos began to emerge from the tree line with the swaggering confidence of bullies and cowards, Doc singled out two and indicated with a jerk of his thumb where Marlowe had disappeared into the Table Rocks.

The two honored ones rushed into the passage wildly, grins splattered across their faces, new ammunition clips in their Uzis. Doc watched them disappear from sight, listened to their voices shouting pursuit—

—heard the sound of Marlowe's gunfire echoing from the passage. In response to which, Doc quietly chuckled to himself:

"He's *there*."

The sounds of returning gunfire from the two Vavelkos pounded like World War II through the mountain air. Doc led his remaining men into the passage at a slower, more deliberate, more deadly pace.

* * *

Jim's strategy—if he could have paused long enough to give it voice—was basic: he let Mara choose a passage, apparently at random, then he would race furiously after her if no one opened fire. At the end of each dash he would stop and try to catch his breath while listening for pursuers' footsteps. As the footsteps drew near, Jim would jump out into the passage and spray his shots in their direction.

Inevitably he saw most of his pursuers jump to the ground as bullets sparked against the stones around them. Jim did not wait to see if he had hit anyone, turning and running immediately to follow Mara down the next passage.

After several minutes of this—and the exhaustion of two ammunition clips—Jim tried another tactic: he scrambled up one of the "cracks in the ceiling" (as Steve had called them). Jim emerged into the open sunlight to run *across* the top of the Table Rocks, leaping over the passages below.

Doc caught on to this move quickly and directed his Vavelkos to fire at anything they saw in the opening overhead. At one point it seemed to Jim that the earth was shooting bullets, spitting them up from the ground as he and Mara ran across. Within a few minutes Jim was forced back down into the passages: Doc himself had climbed up to the top of the Table Rocks—where he was afforded a clear shot at Jim. His first shots missed as he found his range, but they gave Jim warning enough. He practically dived down the first wide crack.

Had Jim the luxury to observe, he would have noticed that the wolf-dog's random twists and turns through the passageways had about them a deliberate sense of purpose unrelated to escaping their hard-pressing pursuers. Unaware that he was being "led," then, Jim stopped in a blind panic when it appeared that he had followed Mara into a dead end!

There was little else to do but make a stand. Jim switched his automatic weapon to single-shot in an attempt to conserve what precious little ammunition he had left, and backed up towards the dead end while facing the open passage he had just exited. He thought wildly for a moment of returning to that passage and shooting his way out—but it was clearly held now by his pursuers. The only cover left him was the large boulder at the end of the dead end: it offered the chance of some cover, at least, better than standing out in the open. Mara had already slid behind the boulder. Jim figured he could squeeze behind as well, then pick off Doc's men one by one as they entered the small chamber that fronted the dead end—at least until Doc arrived. Jim had few illusions that Doc had come unprepared. He remembered the explosion at the cabin: Doc would not hesitate to repeat himself.

Jim fired three random shots down the passage to discourage anyone nearby, then turned his back on the passage and ran for the boulder. As he rounded the edge of the huge stone he saw Mara already standing there—at the entrance to a deep, torchlit shaft!

Bullets striking the stone relieved Jim of the opportunity to wonder at this sudden exit: Doc's men were already in the small chamber, closing in on the boulder.

Jim fired several shots blindly at a sidewall of stone, sending bullets ricocheting wildly about, forcing the Vavelkos to drop to the ground once again. Then he turned and began running at full speed down the hidden shaft.

CHAPTER 25

The Chamber

The torches!—Jim thought frantically as he ran—I have to extinguish the torches! They can see me, but—

His lungs burned with agonizing insistence as he forced his feet to pound down rapidly on the salt-striated stone floor of the shaft. Jim could hear the running feet of Doc and his men behind him, but were they close? The slaps of his own feet echoed in his ears, distorting any perception of distance from his pursuers. Where was Mara? The wolf-dog had run so far ahead of Jim that she was lost in the distance. He thought about grabbing at the torches again—but there was no time, no energy, to stop and raise his arm. To stop: that would be suicide. Were they near? The shaft slanted at a downhill angle. Jim let gravity pull him forward. They had to be tired, too, didn't they? He almost dropped the automatic pistol. Grip it harder!, Jim told himself. That made his shoulders ache. He was using his arms too much. I don't need my arms to run, Jim reminded himself, not for the long distance. Not now. Doc would be using his arms. Doc would be aiming.

Without an intelligent reason to confirm the suspicion, Jim began to twist his body.

Bullets rang across the center of the shaft, striking the walls up ahead, flying through the empty space that had been occupied by Jim's body only a second before.

Then he noticed that the shaft had drastically widened.

Bullets continued to sing through the dark air, but now Jim saw huge stalactites hanging to the floor, columns of hardened minerals to hide behind as he ran deeper into the unknown chambers ahead.

Doc jogged easily at the head of his men: the Vavelkos were out of shape, only the bloodlust of the chase kept them going. They lagged behind, though, and as Doc jogged cautiously out of the shaft and into the stalactite-filled chamber, he paused briefly to let them pull even with him and catch their breaths. He saw Marlowe darting from column to column at the far end of the chamber. Doc nodded to one of the more reliable Vavelkos and allowed the man to unloose a shotgun blast across the empty space. Of course it could not hit Marlowe from this distance, Doc smiled, but they were rabbit hunting now, weren't they? Got to frighten the rabbits a bit to flush them out of hiding.

The shotgun blast echoed through the first chamber, down the connecting tunnel, through second and third chambers—into the Dragon's lair. Another blast followed. Then Mara padded into the lair, dropping to the ground at the White Horse's feet, foam flecking her open mouth, panting heavily. The White Horse's eyes colored drastically. He saw the blind girl turn her face towards him.

"Jim is here . . . your promise."

More sounds of gunfire filtered into the lair. The White Horse snorted nervously. Steve slid off his back and put his face next to the White Horse's muzzle.

"Your promise!" the boy demanded.

Mara felt the hairs on her back rise as the voice whispered fiercely in response:

"The promise was to myself: *they* are *here*!"

The eyes of the White Horse grew red with anger. The boy did not back his head away.

"They are in *my* lair!"

The wolf-dog rose to her feet, nudging the blind girl to do likewise. The White Horse shook his head angrily. He stepped away from the boy, raising his legs high and drop-

ping them in sharp, piercing blows into the layers of gemstones that covered the ground, scattering them about.

Through the many-colored perception of his own eyes,
the White Horse sought contact with the boy's eyes
again—touched. Steve's six-year-old eyes were as angry,
as purely filled with purpose, conscienceless purpose, as
his own.

The White Horse shook his head wildly, then set forth
towards the sound of the increasing gunfire.

Past the skins of defeated dragons past.

Past the Chinese painting of the Black Horse.

Across the floor deep in gems.

The White Horse brushed past Jewel and Steve, gone
from the grotto that was his lair.

The sound of gunfire screamed loudly in his absence.

"Tuan!" Jewel cried.

Steve looked at Jewel for a moment—the wolf-dog was
by her side—then ran madly in pursuit of the White
Horse!

This one's going to come first—or maybe that one—no!

Jim fired a single shot at the moving figure charging at
him. The man fell. The second man charged. Jim fired.
Missed. The man kept coming, firing blindly. Jim fell to
the ground, firing three shots in succession. The second
man fell. The shotgun blasted out from somewhere in the
dark cavern. Jim felt the sting of several pellets pushing
into his left shoulder blade. He ran.

They were nearer now, forcing him back to lower and
lower tunnels and chambers. Doc kept his men
moving—he could care less whether they survived the
chase or not, but he did not want them panicking. He kept
them moving past the bodies of their dead partners. Doc
had taken the shotgun. He found its deep booming explosions more satisfying than the crackling sounds of the automatic weapons. Marlowe would run out of running room
soon, or ammunition. Either way . . .

Jim lined up his shot and squeezed it off: the pursuer
fell. Another took his place, not certain where Jim was,

but charging in the right direction. Jim lined up his shot again, squeezed the trigger—nothing happened. Jim turned and ran deeper into the cavern.

But this second man was faster than Jim. His weapon was empty, too, but he did not want to waste time reloading: he would catch the American on the run and beat him to a pulp with his fists. He grabbed at Marlowe's elbow.

Jim felt the jerk, spun around, and flung his empty weapon into the pursuer's face. The Vavelko's eyes bent back, stunned. Jim pulled loose from the man's weakened grasp and disappeared down a passage leading off the chamber. Passage, hell! It was practically an arched hallway!

As he had done at the entrance to the Table Rocks, at this sign of powerlessness—the empty weapon on the floor—Doc stepped confidently and deliberately into the open. He picked up Marlowe's useless gun. The Vavelkos understood what this meant, too, and started to run in pursuit. Doc held them back.

"No hurry, gentlemen." He looked down at Marlowe's last victory: the Vavelko was sitting on the ground nursing a broken nose. "Why don't you all take this opportunity to reload," he said sarcastically, dropping Marlowe's empty Uzi into the man's lap.

He looked down the passage where Marlowe had temporarily escaped, and set up an echoing taunt:

"You should have taken the money, Mr. Marlowe!"

But it was not the time to enjoy any long-lingering pleasures: with a shrug Doc led his men in a fast-walking pursuit down the passage.

Without the burden of the gun, Jim had thought that he would run faster. But fear and exhaustion had taken their toll. He was stumbling now, practically shuffling his feet as he passed into a new chamber. Jim did not have the energy to notice that this one was filled with carvings, that the ground was embedded with precious stones. Scared and badly winded, he crossed the chamber to find a new, half-lit tunnel. Jim turned into it—

—and tripped face-first to the ground.

He wanted to stay there, stay there with his eyes closed and enjoy the unconsciousness that waited to envelop him. Instead Jim forced his eyes open.

The White Horse was standing over him, stamping its feet in prancing agitation, tossing its head.

Jim heard the many, deliberate footsteps of Doc and his men enter the chamber he had just run from: they were fanning out across the space.

Jim forced himself to his knees.

"Dad!"

Steve's cry pulled Jim out of his brain-numbing exhaustion.

The White Horse began to pace.

Jim looked at his son, realizing:

"You're hiding back there, aren't you—"

Doc noticed the carvings on the chamber walls, the jewels set into the stones beneath his feet. The Vavelkos noticed, too.

"Keep moving," Doc ordered. "We'll come back here." He fell a pace behind the men, let them know that his shotgun was at their backs. "Keep moving!"

Jim could hear the steady cadence of the pursuers' footsteps as they crossed the chamber. Soon they would be entering the tunnel. If they did that, Doc would find the kids sooner or later.

"What the hell . . ." Jim groaned. He knew what must be done. He bent down to his son.

"Steve, go back to Jewel. Hide in any corner—don't make a sound!"

He grabbed hold of the White Horse's long mane—the beast stopped its insistent pacing—then pulled himself onto the animal's back. His son looked very small from such a perspective.

"Steve, I love you. I'll get 'em away from here."

The boy did not move.

"Run!"

Steve turned and ran back into the tunnel. Jim guided the White Horse's head in the opposite direction, towards the chamber. He leaned his head down to put his mouth next to the beast's ear.

"I hope you're fast."

Grasping two handfuls of the horse's mane, Jim rammed his heels into the animal's flanks—but the White Horse took off even faster than he had prodded!

With Jim hanging precariously onto his back, the White Horse emerged from the tunnel just as Doc's line of men were set to converge into it. Those Vavelkos closest to the entrance scattered for protection from the pounding hooves. Jim urged the White Horse to make a break across the chamber—they were stopped abruptly by a line of bullets spattering across the floor at the exit, causing horse and rider to pull up short.

Doc had taken a high position and was covering the chamber exit. His shotgun lay at his feet; the Uzi in his hands continued to pepper the exit.

The White Horse remembered such maneuvers—when men used arrows instead of bullets—but his tactics would work the same for both as long as there were so many men surrounding him at close quarters. Clinging to the animal's back, Jim, too, seemed to understand what needed to be done, as the White Horse turned from the exit and ran around the edge of the chamber, scattering Doc's men and staying too close to them to allow their easy shooting— unless they wanted to shoot one another.

It was only a temporary solution. There was still only one open exit: the tunnel leading to Jewel and Steve.

Doc stopped firing, signaled his men to follow his lead, as he called out:

"Good afternoon, Mr. Marlowe!"

Jim did not intend to answer. Instead, he prodded the White Horse to continue pacing back and forth before the tunnel entrance.

Doc set aside his Uzi and picked up the shotgun. He liked the feel of the heavy weapon. He stepped down from his high position and walked out to the center of the chamber.

"Get off the horse, Mr. Marlowe. Why waste such an animal?"

But Doc was no longer covering the other exit. With a "Hey!" Jim galloped the White Horse directly towards that escape.

Doc lifted up his shotgun and blasted.

He had not bothered to aim—and the White Horse took the full brunt of the shotgun blast in his face, causing him to rear up, back onto his hind legs—then fall!

Jim felt the horse take the blast, then knew that he was being flung through the air. He crashed against the tunnel entrance, stunned. He was uncertain whether he was conscious or not: although he was certain that he saw Doc's men closing in on him, he felt blackness, too, taking away his eyesight. He could barely make out the White Horse lying near him, beads of red blood covering the animal's face, sides panting heavily, head lowered . . .

Suddenly, quickly, the White Horse snapped his head up!

A shower of precious stones flew from his face, where the drops of blood had been, streaking across the air to land at the feet of Doc's men.

Even as the White Horse rose, the transformation began—to the frozen disbelief of the Vavelkos. Only, now there was more to the Dragon: his white scales were studded with color, gemstones clinging to his sides. His eyes flashed with an ancient power: they were in *his* lair! His eyes changed color rapidly, noting with approval his reflection in the crystal walls of the chamber as he stretched his wings, then folded them with a snap! A slash of flame lightning burst across the chamber. *THEY WERE IN HIS LAIR!* The dragon's long, thick tail glided along the floor, scattering the gemstones in a stinging spray against the men's faces. The Dragon craned his serpentine, muscular neck to hover over the prone figure of the boy's father.

"Not you," Jim heard whispered through his unconsciousness.

Doc, too, heard the words, watched the impossible happen, on the border between evaluation of the situation and fear.

The White Dragon, whole and complete, remained facing away from the men, his eyes on the boy's father, gave the pursuers a moment to run before turning his attention back to them. At that opportunity, only Doc had the presence of mind to dive behind a large column. The Dragon twisted his head around to face the line of men, stretching to his full height.

The Vavelkos stood rooted to their places, caught between the half-crazy rush of excitement and half-paralyzed with fear. They stared at the creature before them, beginning to finger their weapons.

A chamber action clicked.

An ammunition clip was snapped in.

The White Dragon stared at the men, their weapons in hand, facing him like . . .

Knights of the Order emerging from the tree line atop their horses: in battle line, facing the Dragon, stepping past the writhing body of the dying Black Horse. Their lances and swords at the ready, they walked steadily towards the beast.

Lulled by the Dragon's motionlessness, the Vavelkos began to feel confident, raising their weapons.

At the rear of the chamber, Doc crawled along the ground, sliding towards a position that would put him behind the Dragon.

Tuan turned his head slowly, gracefully, to view his adversaries. The Vavelkos heard the quiet, whispering voice:

"You do have a chance. There *is* a heart. I have to tell you that."

But, with that final phrase, the Dragon's tail whipped out—striking down two of the men!

The Vavelkos began shooting wildly, crying animal-like sounds, spraying bullets on the Dragon's body, spreading apart as the Dragon reared up to his full height, his wings outstretched. Fire billowed from his mouth—a man cried out in agony.

Fire, and more fire, gushed forth from the Dragon's mouth and nostrils. The Vavelkos screamed louder, shooting crazily. Still more fire filled the chamber, until the Dragon's head could no longer be seen through the flames, until the roar of the flames became so loud that it obscured the dying cries of the men, the dying sounds of gunfire, the dying memories of horses and knights. Until the Dragon's crying, hate-filled eyes saw only a chamber turned red with flame.

He did not see the boy's father crawl, delirious, down the tunnel. He did not see Doc, minutes later, rush down the same tunnel without a second look back at the fate of his men.

CHAPTER 26
The Lair

Jim could not have said how he found Steve and Jewel. He did not recall crawling for a dozen minutes on his stomach—although his shirt was shredded as proof of that—nor could he remember rising to his feet and stumbling blindly down the tunnel, his eyes closed all the while. Somewhere along the tunnel his shuffling steps had attracted Mara's attention: the wolf-dog had abandoned Steve and Jewel to go out and retrieve her master. Jim was not aware of any of this. Or if he was, if what he remembered was what he *thought* he saw, then he was crazy. He was certain, for example, that gemstones were sparkling like fire beneath his feet as he followed Mara into a grotto, where Jewel and Steve rushed over to him.

"Dad!" the boy cried.

Jim felt himself fall into a soft pile of loose stones, then knew that Jewel was moving his head onto her lap. He had to tell them about what he saw.

"There was ... I rode it ..."

Jim could not open his eyes. He wanted to sleep.

"It was Tuan," he heard Jewel say. "He will help us. He will help us."

"I have." Jim heard the same whispered voice that had spoken to him in the chamber. His eyes opened now without effort.

"Tuan! It's Tuan, Dad!" he saw his son cry as Steve

rushed towards the grotto entrance to greet the Dragon gliding in. Jim refused to believe the hallucination.

Mara, too, padded across the gemstone carpet to greet the Dragon, kneeling before the beast and licking at his claws. The Dragon bowed his huge head in acknowledgment, then curved his neck to survey the girl caressing the man. He bent his neck to an even more extreme angle to see the boy.

"You can help me, boy. There is a pain in my side." Tuan unfolded a wing, revealing a dripping line of rubies on his flank. "I think that one of them may have actually hurt me."

His many-colored eyes saw the blind girl start, felt satisfaction at her concern.

"You are hurt! Where?!" She lowered the man's head to the ground and rose toward the sound of the voice.

"Don't move!" Jim ordered, holding her hand in tense horror at the sight before him.

The Dragon ignored the man's reaction. He used his head to point out the wound to the boy, used his words to reassure the girl.

"It is small. It is for small boys."

The wound was on his flank, near the wall—hidden from the sight of the older humans.

"Here," Steve heard the whispered instructions. "Mara will know what to do."

Mara rose and stepped over to the indicated place. Steve walked widely around the front of the Dragon to follow—to be stopped by Jim's strong order:

"Steve! Don't go closer! Don't move!"

"Dad, Tuan's hurt," the boy matter-of-factly replied as he ignored his father's command.

"Steve!"

Jewel heard the fear in Jim's voice.

"Jim, why do you—"

Her question was cut short by Tuan's voice.

"There are more of your pursuers here." The Dragon raised his head in sense of something. "You are not safe."

Jewel protested: "They would not—"

"I will smell them and find them."

"They are here." Tai Ching and Alta stepped from behind a curtain of dragons' skins. Jewel recognized the pace of Alta's footsteps, the sound of her foot against ground.

"Mother!" the blind girl whispered.

Alta heard. She consciously avoided looking at Jewel. Tai Ching, carrying his loaded crossbow at the ready, walked calmly to an open position in front of—but not near—the Dragon. He nodded with respect to the Dragon as he spoke:

"I had always wanted to meet the magic ones, since I was a boy: the dragon on parade, the alchemist with his dream powder"—without taking his eyes off the Dragon he nodded towards Alta—"the *witch* with her eyes . . ."

"You are holding a weapon." The words cut across the lair like a scornful wind.

Tai Ching looked at his weapon and answered with mock naïveté:

"Why, yes—I am."

Alta allowed herself to look at Jewel now, gazing into the girl's blank eyes, hoping for a quick death to the girl and the Dragon.

Tuan turned his head to look at Alta. A weariness tinged the next words heard.

"It was neither of you I sensed. There is another."

The Dragon pointedly allowed himself to crane his neck away from the danger of Tai Ching and Alta, twisting his head towards the entrance to his lair. Suddenly, from the shadow at the entrance, Doc burst into the grotto, frightened by the Dragon's stare. He rolled as if ducking gunshots aimed overhead, then ran hard and direct towards the fallen Jim and Jewel. In one swift movement Doc used his automatic pistol to club Jim in the side of the head while roughly grabbing Jewel with his free hand.

"I saw you!" he cried out frantically to the Dragon, pointing his gun into Jewel. "Whatever you are, you won't hurt her!"

"Doc! You survived!" Tai Ching shouted with the same mockery of delight with which he had greeted the Dragon.

Doc jerked his attention over to the Chinaman.

"What the hell are you doing with this thing, Ching?"

The Dragon let his head hover between the two.

"Let go of the girl!"

At his recognition of weakness on the part of the monster, Doc allowed himself to relax a bit. His "professional" smile returned. he nodded in appreciation of the Dragon's power to Tai Ching.

"Did you see what this thing can do?"

"No, I missed it—but thank you for distracting him for me."

"You bastard! You knew—"

"Let go of the girl!"

Alta saw death in every eye, watched the shouting match with hungry anticipation.

Doc shoved the gun into Jewel even harder as he yelled up at the Dragon:

"I'll let her go when I'm gone—this is my passport!" He jabbed the gun into the blind girl's side, making her cry out in pain. "Try to burn me and she goes, too!"

Tuan's eyes welled up into a kaleidoscope of emotion: the Black Horse reared up in pain, mortally wounded, crying out in her agony.

Gracefully, almost dancelike, the Dragon swung his long neck to face Doc and Jewel. He turned Doc to stone in an instant.

"You will not die. You will still *think*!" the words hissed into the stone.

A heartbeat later, Tai Ching's arrow pierced Tuan's heart.

The Dragon froze in mid-motion, turning to face his murderer—froze and then, with a shudder, collapsed.

Everything was very quiet for a long moment: only the sounds of Tai Ching's movements, readying an arrow in his crossbow, just in case. Jim breathed shallowly, still unconscious. Jewel knelt on the ground where she had fallen, released from Doc's grasp by Tuan's dying act. Alta stood waiting, anticipating, seeing but not hearing the small, dying breaths coming from the Dragon.

It was Tai Ching who spoke first—when he was certain that the Dragon was no longer a threat. He addressed his remarks to the stone that now stood behind Jewel:

"Thanks, Doc." He turned his attention to Alta. "Well, did everything happen that you wanted? Any *change*?"

He said these words with cruel obviousness: it was apparent from Alta's disorientation that nothing *had* happened. She answered Tai Ching in a hoarse whisper, staring at Jewel:

"*She* has to die, too!" Alta looked to Tai Ching to finish it.

Jewel turned her head at the words, to face her "mother."

Tai Ching considered them both. Finally, shrugging, he indicated the crossbow and laid it on the ground, saying with matter-of-fact simplicity:

"Then do it."

He turned towards the Dragon, pulling out the long-bladed Indonesian kris from his belt.

Alta stepped up to the crossbow, looking at it in a panic, then looking over at Jewel. The blind girl could hear her spastic breaths.

"Yes. Go ahead, *mother*," Jewel drawled sarcastically.

But Alta did not move. Tai Ching nodded.

"Let me count the teeth. There is always later for her."

He walked up to the Dragon's head, watching carefully the few shallow breaths coming from the beast's mouth. Satisfied that there was no threat from the Dragon, Tai Ching threw his kris into the gem-strewn ground, point-first. He squatted down before the head and began to count the teeth.

The low growl of the wolf-dog caused him to stop his count and look up.

Steve and Mara stood atop the Dragon. The wolf-dog stared intently at Tai Ching, the growl deep in her throat. The boy carried the same look of hatred in his eyes.

"No," he said simply.

The last thing Tai Ching was to see was the glint on

Mara's teeth, followed by the animal's heavy body hurtling towards him.

Tai Ching's death cry ripped through the lair, clawing Alta and Jewel's attention apart, causing them to turn towards the sound in alarm.

Steve watched, eyes dark and filled with the anger of centuries, listening to the short, fierce sounds. A tearing sound ended the wolf-dog's efforts. A final gasping moan shuddered from Tai Ching.

Steve looked up at Alta. Mara raised her bloodied mouth.

"Go away," the boy commanded.

"NO!" Alta cried out. *"NOTHING CHANGED!"* She looked about her in fear and hopelessness, from Jewel to Steve, from Steve to the unconscious Jim, trying to explain to no one and everyone in a now-quiet voice:

"Nothing changed."

She turned to Jewel one last time, looked at the girl she had brought up—and had abandoned beyond all hope of recovery this day. Then Alta brought herself erect and left.

The sound of her footsteps fading down the distant tunnel mingled with Jewel's weeping, to be joined by the soft groans sighing from Jim as he tried to open his eyes—only to have the gentle fingertips of the girl press them closed.

"No! Don't open them!" she sobbed quietly. "Don't! You will get better. You have to. I thought you were dead. I thought . . . Tuan is dead. Why? . . . why? And then I saw the blood on your head, and I thought you were dead, too! But you are not, Jim, I can see your eyes—you will be better! I can see that, I can . . . I can . . ."

And Jewel realized that she, indeed, could see. Could see. Could see her tears dripping wet across Jim's face! Could see his beautiful, swollen, bruised face! Jewel wiped at that tear-streaked face with her hand, looking at Jim's face in wonder.

"A small miracle," the whisper of a breeze floated through the Lair, "in every death."

The weak words touched her ears softly, causing Jewel

to interrupt her wondrous introduction to Jim Marlowe and the world. She turned her head towards the sound.

She saw the small boy sitting there—Steve—a furry animal by his side—Mara?—a monstrous beast's head in the boys' lap . . .

"Tuan?"

His head held tightly by the small boy, the Dragon's eyes glinted, faded.

"You can see, yes?"

The colors of the eyes changed to a deep, black obsidian. Tuan died.

EPILOGUE

Dinner

At very elegant restaurants, white-coated waiters move past black-coated maître d's without a hint of acknowledgment. Rich, deep-colored tapestries cover the walls. There is a warm hum to conversations. Frank Brown preferred it that way. The Old World way. No five-starred celebrity chefs hovering about crowded tables and insisting that excellent food compensated for incompetent service. Service and excellence, to Frank Brown's mind, were standards that went hand in glove.

Karita stood at the entrance to the dining area. Her beautiful face fit in with the surroundings, but her tired demeanor, overcoat, and traveler's clothes contrasted with the decor. She surveyed the dining room with a purpose, undeterred by the insistent maître d' at her elbow whispering his urgent suggestions that she telephone from the lobby and have the desired party meet her outside. She found the object of her search, of her journey from Karistan.

Karita allowed the maître d' to lead her past the other diners, knowing full well that the son of a bitch had known where Frank Brown was sitting all along, until they arrived at Frank Brown's table.

Brown was dining alone, an enticing and colorful meal set out before him in delicate portions. At the maître d's approach he looked up from a tantalizing cold asparagus soup and saw the blond-haired woman. Brown waived the maître d' away: he could always be summoned later.

"Yes? Do I know you?"

Karita remained standing.

"What day is it?" she asked.

"What day is it? The day?"

"Yes. Please, I have been traveling. I don't know the time."

Brown nodded to accept the explanation.

"Tuesday," he informed her.

Karita pulled an envelope from her pocket and held it out to Brown. It bore the embossed return address of the TransContinental Hotel, Vavel, Karistan.

"Then this is for you."

Brown looked at the finger-smudged envelope dubiously.

"It's from Doc."

Brown took the envelope, motioning for the woman to sit down.

"Please, here, please," he waved with a distracted air.

Karita sat down across the table from Frank Brown. She did not remove her coat, nor did she touch anything on the table in front of her. Rather, she let her eyes wander across the table.

Past the half-eaten aspic.

Doc had not met her across the border from Karistan.

The wineglass was untouched.

She had waited an extra day.

Thin slices of lemon floated distractedly about the finger bowl.

None of the bar-recruited Vavelkos had returned to the city.

A partridge had been penetrated by a knife, its juices running out across Brown's plate. A moment later, Doc's letter slipped from Frank Brown's fingers and fell across the plate. The expensive-bond TransContinental stationery sopped up the juice like a sponge.